I'M YOURS

S. TAYLOR

GARDEN AVENUE PRESS

I'm Yours by S. Taylor

Copyright © 2019, S. Taylor

Garden Avenue Press

Atlanta, Georgia

ISBN: 978-1-940636-75-7 (Ebook edition)

ISBN: 978-1-940636-79-5 (Paperback edition)

This book is a work of fiction. All names, characters, locations, and incidents are products of the author's imagination, or have been used fictitiously. Any resemblance to actual persons living or dead, locales, or events is entirely coincidental. No part of this e-book may be reproduced or shared by any electronic or mechanical means, including but not limited to printing, file sharing, and e-mail, without prior written permission from S. Taylor.

www.gardenavenuepress.com

1

TREVOR

"Oh my God—oh, Trevor, I'm close, baby, do that, do that," says the half-naked female whose name I can't remember.

Do that, do that? Shit, I'm not doing anything. I'm only half erect and it's taking all my concentration to give her that much. Her screaming is annoying. I'm a big man—and I mean all over—but it can't be that intense. I'm not even thrusting.

"Oh God yes, Trevor, I'm coming... I'm coming!" she screams.

Just come already! She needs to hurry the fuck up before she's disappointed when I toss her ass off my dick. *You can't keep doing this shit, Trev.*

Honestly, it's not what's-her-name's fault. I've been engaging in meaningless encounters for... well... fucking forever. I sift through the clutter of faces in my memory, only remembering certain details, all of which are of no consequence.

"Wow, that was amazing."

Were my eyes even open? Hell, did I doze off? Amazing, huh? This woman must be drunk, but that's not possible. I picked her up in the only place resembling a coffee shop out here in the middle of Comoros. This shit is so mundane, I don't even remember what I said to get her back to my room.

She climbs from the bed and walks her bare ass to the bathroom. I toss the condoms in the trash can next to the nightstand. My thoughts go back to the woman in my bathroom—Debbie... Kathy... Pam... no, it's Jackie. What a waste of my time this little encounter was. Jacking off would have been more pleasurable. I haven't been into sex for so long, I've forgotten what genuine attraction feels like. It's only gotten worse since my thirty-fourth birthday.

"I'm off," what's-her-name says.

I nod and sit up, swinging my legs to the side of the bed—still naked, anxious for her to leave so I can shower and sleep.

"If you're ever in town again, call. I'd love to do this again." She hands me a slip of paper.

I smile at her, not wanting to give her any hopes that I'll call one day, but I also don't want to be an asshole to her either. She walks out, and I lock the door before making my way to the bathroom, looking down at the slip of paper. *Nancy, damn, I wasn't even close.* I crumble the paper with Nancy's name and number written on it before tossing it into the wastebasket.

I remove the hair tie from my wrist and secure my long sandy-brown dreads in a knot atop my head. As I step under the spray of hot water, every muscle in my body relaxes, and I moan my approval. Once I'm clean from head to toe, I crawl back into bed and close my eyes.

The banging I hear isn't in my head. I slowly open my eyes and stare at the chipping paint on the ceiling before I turn toward the source of my disturbance. I check the time. I've been asleep for a few hours. I hope it's not Nancy.

"Mr. Duncan? Hello, Mr. Duncan, I have a message for you." The innkeeper bangs the door again. "I was told it was urgent and you need to call right away." Scrubbing my face, I attempt to work energy into my body as I stand. I throw on some cargo shorts and a navy T-shirt, slip on my worn leather flip-flops before I grab the knob and pull open the door. He hands me the slip of paper, motioning for me to follow him to the front room. "You can use my phone in the office."

Nodding and half-listening, I stare at a name I haven't seen in seven years. I swallow the panic rising inside my gut and follow him to the small room and dial.

After a receptionist's friendly greeting, I say, "Trevor Duncan, for Jackson Marsh."

It's only a moment before the call is transferred to my family's attorney. "Trevor, thank you for calling me back so soon. I was hoping this message found its way to you."

"No problem, Jack. You chose a good day to reach out."

"Well, I wish I didn't have to call, but... well, I have some news."

Before he can deliver the blow, I stop him with, "When did it happen?"

"God, this is hard—I hate to tell you this, but..."

"When, Jackson?" My throat closes, and heat rushes through me and burns my eyes.

What I was feeling wasn't nothing. *Braden!* I scream his name in my head and close my eyes as I listen to Jack inform me that my brother and his wife were involved in a hit-and-run nearly two months ago. They were both pronounced dead on arrival at the hospital, and Jack has been trying to track me down since then. Tears slide down my face when I drop my head in my hand, feeling like such a selfish bastard.

"You said it was him and his wife..."

"Yes, luckily Adeline was at school. She is doing well, considering what she's been through."

"Where is she?"

"That's the thing. In your brother's will, you're named as Adeline's legal guardian. You're the only family she has."

The weight of his statement hits me with the force of a semi-truck. *She's all I have now too. I need to get to her, make sure she's okay, but where is she?*

"Is Adeline in foster care?" I ask, fully understanding how the system works for children with no one.

"Yes and no. After the accident, I got a judge to grant emergency temporary custody to a family friend of mine. Adeline could have gone into the system, but Ms. Jordan was kind enough to take her in until I could get word to you."

"Thank God for angels," I say, remembering those were my mother's words.

"I need you in my office ASAP. Your brother gave further instructions regarding Adeline's care and her future. There are also financial matters we need to settle. When can you return to the States?"

As best as possible, I think over my obligations. I've been registered as a volunteer supervisor for the last ten years with Northern Star, an organization dedicated to improving living conditions in third world countries. "Two, maybe three weeks. I'll call you as soon as I land."

"Sure, I understand. I'll plan on meeting in two weeks then."

"Thanks, and can you give me Ms. Jordan's contact information? I'd like to reach out, check up on Adeline. I want to let her know I'll be there for her soon."

I jot down her full name, address, and cell phone number. I end the call with Jackson and immediately call Ms. Peggy Jordan, after checking the time. It's late here, on this island off the coast of East Africa which would make it morning in Georgia. *I hope this isn't too early.* I know next to nothing about kids. I've never met my niece and don't know what all she knows about me. I would love to hear her voice, but Braden and I sound so alike over the phone, I may upset her. I'll just keep this call short, then I can start getting my shit together.

"Hello?—that's enough, honey, put a little butter, sweetheart—This is Peggy—orange juice coming right up—I'm sorry, hello? This is Peggy Jordan."

Ms. Jordan's voice strikes me speechless. It's soft tone and sleepy rasp warms my insides, a response my body has never felt before. I'm confused as to why my body is choosing now to wake up, but I listen, hoping to hear her breathy hello again. Instead I'm snapped from my trance by a sweet giggle followed by, "This is good pancakes, Peggy."

Taking a deep breath, I push back the sudden punch to my gut. Adeline sounds so happy, so little. I exhale before finding my voice. "Hello, Ms. Jordan, I'm Trevor Duncan. I believe you have my niece? I was given your number by Jackson Marsh."

"Oh, God, yes, Mr. Duncan." She goes quiet and then whispers, "Give me a sec." I hear what sounds like cooking pans being placed in the sink then running water. "Addie, I'll be right back, sweetheart. Finish your breakfast and we'll dress for the park after."

I listen but can't hear a reply. She must have left the room. "Ms. Jordan?"

"Yes, I'm sorry for that, Mr. Duncan. I promised Adeline last week we would go to the water park today."

"So she's good?"

"Yes, she's perfect." I can hear she's smiling, and I try to imagine what it looks like. "Mr. Marsh informed me it may take some time to get word to you, but I wasn't expecting it to be nearly two months. Don't get me wrong, I've enjoyed having Adeline with me. I'm just shocked you went unaware of the situation for so long. I'm so sorry for your loss."

"Thank you, and thanks for caring for Adeline. She's been through so much."

"It's my pleasure."

There's that smile in her voice again. I try harder to picture the smile that would match her beautiful voice, and come up with nothing. I'm so overwhelmed with curiosity, I almost ask her to describe herself. But I'm saved from making a fool of myself when she says, "I'll be right there, Addie. Let me finish this call and I'll help you." She sighs.

I wait for the next words spoken in that sweet voice of hers.

Strangely, her voice calms me, and I want more of it. When I think she won't give me what I need, I help her out. "Problem?"

"Well… it's been hard for Adeline. For the most part, she's getting along great, but… she's still so afraid of being left. When I'm not in her sight, she panics."

"Fuck," I whisper, fighting my emotions. Her constant fear lights the fire of urgency inside me. I clear my throat before apologizing for my language.

"No worries, I'm the one who's sorry." I hear compassion in her voice. "I shouldn't have told you that, not when you have such a long travel ahead of you. I don't think you need that worry placed on you right now. We'll talk more when you arrive, which will be…?"

"Two weeks, give or take. I have to settle some things with work." *I wish I were there now.*

"Okay, I'll see you in two weeks."

"I look forward to it."

"Right. Goodbye, Mr. Duncan."

"See you soon, Ms. Jordan."

I hang up the phone and head back to my room, where I quickly grab my belongings to start the necessary steps to Adeline… and to Peggy Jordan.

∽

MY BUSINESS AFFAIRS took a week wrapping up, and now I'm boarding a flight home. I left Jackson a message I'll be able to meet sooner than planned. I locate my seat and stow my duffle bag in the overhead compartment. I haven't been home in seven years—not since my father's funeral. The flight will be long, which I hate. There'll be hours for me to think. That visit home was the last time Braden and I exchanged words, and his were harsh.

The thought of that night fills me with regret. Braden and I had a terrible argument where he called me selfish and accused me of being just like our father. 'You can run from it all you want, Trev, but running will never change who you really are," he said.

My father and I were never on good terms, ever in my life. Even now when I try to remember good times, I only picture my mother's face. I should've held onto my brother instead of walking away, but him cursing, calling me selfish, stung. Going home to him not being there will… will…

My thoughts halt because nothing good will come of them. So, instead of beating myself up for the next several hours, I decide to figure out how I'm going to raise a little girl, a wonderful, talented, smart little girl I've been told. I've called Ms. Jordan a couple times to keep her updated on my progress, check in on Adeline, and also to hear her beautiful voice.

I reach for my worn leather wallet and pull out the family photo Braden mailed me three years ago. I've never met my brother's family. He married his wife Traci a few years after our Father died, and in this picture, Adeline is about two years old. She looks like my mother and that makes me smile. Before her lost battle with cancer—Braden and I were high school juniors—my mom promised she would always be with us and seeing her eyes and smile part of Adeline's features warms my heart. I slip the photo back in its place in my wallet and allow this comforting warmth to calm me. I close my eyes, welcoming sleep.

∼

I FORGOT how much I hate the smell of Jackson's office. It doesn't smell unpleasant, it's the memories I associate with the spicy scent, my mother's will reading, my father's will reading, and now Braden's. Shifting in my seat, I fight the urge to run, but it's not just me anymore. I have to think of a kid now.

I've never given a family much thought. I think about my life and how I've lived it since leaving home at twenty-one. I help people, travel, and I'm free. I found fulfillment in my work volunteering in third world countries, living for months or possibly years at a time in one place, providing whatever is needed to better the conditions. For the last two years we've been building a medical clinic.

But would a family be the worst thing for me? A beautiful wife to come home to, a daughter to love, spoil, and protect. It would beat the lonely life I've carved out for myself.

"Great to see you Trevor." Jackson enters his office with a stack of folders tucked under his arm. I stand and extend my hand and realize how many years older Jackson looks from the last time we were together. "We have a lot to address, so I'll jump right into it," Jackson says. He drops the folders on his desk and takes his seat. I do the same, but I'm so nervous I wish I could stand for this.

"I'm all ears," I say. I lean forward like I'm eager for what's to come, but this is the only way to keep my ass in this chair.

"Wonderful to hear. Let's get started."

∽

I'M SO FUCKED.

The meeting with Jackson has my head spinning. I run down the list of important details. First, all Braden's assets go to Adeline, even my father's estate. That's cool, I didn't want it seven years ago and I sure don't want it now. I can't even step foot in the place, reason why I cut the wheel right and bring my rental car to a stop in front the small two bedroom home I found on the internet for rent.

In person it looks much older and more neglected then the picture from the website. I throw the car in park. This will have to do for now. I promised Alexander Duncan over thirteen years ago I would never step foot in his home again. One promise I plan on keeping. My father was a hard man to love and we never got along. He was a corrupt alcoholic who neglected his children and cheated on his wife. But to hear Braden tell it, our father was a law-abiding citizen, hardworking business man, a man of honor, a faithful husband and loving father.

Braden and I are identical twins, but very different men. He would jump through hoops to please the old man, and I couldn't care fucking less what he wanted of me. I wasn't surprised to learn he took up residence in that miserable mansion.

Secondly, Braden wants me to legally adopt Adeline. Apparently, I was his first and only choice to take in his daughter should anything happen to him. It seems as if his wife wanted nothing to do with Adeline.

Am I really surprised to learn his wife Traci isn't Adeline's mother? No. Alexander's bad habits had to go somewhere, right? Jackson presented me with Adeline's birth certificate. She was born in Las Vegas, Nevada. Her birth mother's name is Denise Davis. This Denise woman must have been a real piece of work to sign away her maternal rights for a the amount of five hundred thousand dollars.

But where I'm royally fucked, is that I'm now expected to take my place as CEO of The Golden Temple, my father's beloved casino, located on the Vegas strip. A responsibility I ran from thirteen years ago.

My tension is building. I inhale and blow out my stress before I unfold my big frame from the economy size rental and walk up to the house to greet the man clad in a black suit standing on the small weather-beaten porch to sign my rental agreement.

2

PEGGY

I can't think of a better way to wake in the morning.

I hear the sweet music of Adeline's giggle again, but I still pretend I'm sleeping. I feel another light tap atop my right hand which I have resting on my pillow next to my face. I risk a quick peek, don't see her little face in front of me, and know she's hiding in her comfortable place, under my bed.

She sneaks in in the middle of the night and crawls under there. When she made that a regular habit, I tried to convince her it was okay to climb in my bed, that the floor was hard and cold. She told me that she was a big girl and didn't need to sleep with anyone. She doesn't like to be alone, but she still struggles to be independent. I accepted that, so I set her up a pallet with quilts and pillows, so she could be comfortable and warm while being a big girl.

She pops up like a jack-in-the-box. Her short curls are crazy on top her head, a few coils falling over her dark eyes. "Good morning, Peggy."

"Good morning, squirt. How is it under there?"

"Great!" she shouts, raising her little arms.

My heart swells. I'm going to miss this little girl. I already feel lost.

"Pancakes?" she asks.

Wrinkling my nose, I pretend to contemplate her request.

"Please, please, please with lots of honey and berries?" She rests her chin in her palms, smiling at me. She knows what she's doing. I've given in to plenty of her requests thanks to that look.

"Okay. Pancakes it is."

I climb out of bed and rush through my morning grooming. Staring in the mirror, I close my eyes and try not to think of Adeline Duncan leaving me. This little fantasy, this peek into the life that could have been—if I wasn't damaged, chasing every man who ever showed interest in me away—will end. Goodbye to homemade pancake breakfasts and morning gardening. Goodbye to afternoon naps. Goodbye messy arts and crafts and trips to the farmers' market for fresh fruits and veggies. Goodbye to laughter, to love, to Adeline. In a few days, Adeline's uncle will come take her away.

I haven't told her about him. I didn't want her hopes up in case he changes his mind. We've spoken on the phone a couple times, where he's asked all about her and occasionally slid in a question about me. I don't believe he will abandon her, but these things can happen.

I splash hot water over my face to scrub away the looming dread. With my face washed and teeth brushed, I strip out of my nightshirt and slip on a pair of white cotton shorts and a white muscle shirt. I didn't bother with a bra, because it's just Adeline and me. Besides, it's Saturday morning and we have a full day of doing everything and nothing at all.

Scooping her up, I make my way to the kitchen. The floorboards crack and squeak under the slightest weight, and I smile with happy memories, from before my parents died. The sound always brings me comfort, as everything in my childhood home does.

My house sits on an acre of land, so it's nice and private. I love summers in Savannah, weekends full of endless possibilities, but mostly, how peaceful my life is. I plop her on one of the barstools at my large island and slide over her coloring books and art supply caddy so she can stay busy while I cook.

I pop in the CD soundtrack for Disney's *The Princess and the Frog*. I get to work dumping ingredients in the mixing bowl and adjusting the settings before I turn it on. While the mixer goes, I place a few strips of bacon in the skillet, place a lid on top, and move to the fruit and veggie drawer in the refrigerator. I remove some blueberries and strawberries and wash a few that I dump in a bowl with a dusting of powdered sugar and slide it in front of Adeline. She smiles at me and pops a berry in her mouth.

I turn up the music and open the French doors, welcoming in the morning breeze. I dance over to the cook top, flip the bacon before turning off the mixer, and pour the mixture in a large pan, peeking over my shoulder as Adeline pops the last berry in her mouth.

"Go wash your sticky hands please, then put away your crafts."

Adeline carries out my request, and I place her empty bowl in the sink and watch her skip from the kitchen. I set the knobs to medium heat and dance across the kitchen floor to the refrigerator for the carton of orange juice. I pour her a glass, but before I set it and her placemat on the table, I speed over to the stove and flip the pancakes.

"Perfect." I turn off the heat on the bacon and grab a paper towel to absorb the grease.

"Something sure smells good," a deep voice booms over the music.

I'm startled mid-lift with a hot strip of bacon, and grease hits my bare thigh. I yelp from the sting of the hot grease and grab a dishtowel, then I rush to the sink and wet the ends. As I bend forward for a better look at my wound, strong hands hold mine steady before taking the towel. I distinctly smell lavender, and my mouth waters.

The room fills with an earsplitting scream. The stranger and I turn to see Adeline's face is as white as a sheet. She's standing in the doorway and then runs from the room as if hell is on her heels.

"Adeline!" I call.

I turn to the stranger still kneeling at my feet, his warm hand around my upper thigh as he presses the towel to my burned skin.

"Who…?" is about all I can articulate.

I should be fighting and screaming because of the intruder in my home, but strangely, I don't feel panicked because his voice is familiar and *he* looks so familiar, but I can't recall where I know him from. His sandy-brown dreads are tied back from his face. Three or four rest over his shoulder. With his light brown hair, hazel eyes, and toasted brown complexion, he could rival the beauty of the Greek sun god, and he's kneeling at my feet, groping my thigh. Our eyes lock, and my flesh heats to an alarmingly high temperature.

"The open doors don't mean you are welcome to enter my home," I manage to say after finding my voice and attempting to lift his hand from my leg. "Who in the hell are you?"

"Trevor Duncan. I presume you're Peggy Jordan."

He presumes correctly, of course. He's early and at my damn house, in my damn kitchen. I had at least a few more days left with Adeline! *What the fuck, and why is he so fucking gorgeous?*

"You're… you're…"

"Pleased to meet you too." He smiles.

"Early. I was going to say early. You don't know how to ring the doorbell? Or better yet, know how to call first?"

"So you're not pleased?" He smiles and my flesh heats. "I called but there was no answer. I left a message saying I was close and would drop by. Also I did ring the bell and knocked. I heard the music—"

"And you decide to break and enter instead?" I try another attempt to remove his hand. I'm feeling too warm in here and my reaction to him is annoying.

He smiles again. "Breaking and entering? Not quite."

"You startled me! I burned my leg, and let's not forget you frightened the hell out of your niece."

I clamp my lips shut so I don't admit my first feeling was arousal, and holy shit is it powerful. I want nothing more than to open my legs and spread my thighs so he can move that hand to my aching center and give me some relief. *Why is this man so fucking gorgeous?*

"My apologies, Ms. Jordan."

He removes the towel, and what he does next almost makes me faint. He licks his bottom lip—his beautiful, full bottom lip—and presses his moistened mouth to my thigh, planting a soft kiss to my mild burn.

I gasp at the inappropriate contact and bite down hard on my lip to stifle a moan. He stands at his full height, and he dwarfs me. He's wearing trousers paired with a white button-down shirt under a tan sports jacket that hugs his muscular chest and arms. He looks as if he stepped off the cover of a men's fashion spread.

Not knowing what to do with myself, I step back, attempting to clear my head. "I should check on Adeline. We weren't expecting anyone. You startled us both."

"I freaked her out more than you realize. I'm her father's identical twin, I don't think she was expecting to see her father's face in the middle of your kitchen. My brother and I hadn't spoken in several years. I can only conclude by her reaction, my brother never spoke of me much, if at all, to his daughter."

That's it, where I remember seeing his face. "I know, Adeline arrived with a box of keepsakes and a photo album was among the items. I've seen some pictures. Please make yourself comfortable. I was making breakfast." *Of course you were. Stupid much, Peggy?* "What I'm saying—"

"Is that you want me to join you for... breakfast?" He smiles at me, and I'm one hundred percent sure that breakfast was not what he meant, And that comment only is enough to put me off, but I can't seem to help the inappropriately naughty thoughts invading my mind.

My breathing accelerates. With the rise and fall of my chest, I can feel the beat of my pulse and I know I'm as red as a strawberry. His eyes slowly move down my body. I feel the ache of my hard nipples, and I flush even deeper when I remember I'm not wearing a bra. I quickly turn my back to him, completely mortified, and take a few deep breaths to calm my body's erratic impulses.

"I'll be back with Adeline. I'm sure she's hiding in my bedroom."

"I'll come with you."

"No!" I face him again with my hands up to emphasize that he needs to stay put.

To my surprise, my raised hands rest, palms open, on his shirt-clad abs. I was unaware he'd closed the distance between us. My stare is transfixed on my hands as I imagine his abs exposed to me, his smooth brown flesh peeking from between my fingers. I stretch my fingers out and his muscles coil, jumping under my touch. I sigh, longing to snuggle against them. My mouth waters for a taste. A low growl reverberates from him and seeps into me through my hands.

I yank away my hands and cast my eyes downward, afraid of what he may see in them or what I will see in his. "Not necessary. I'll return with Adeline. Just stay here, Mr. Duncan." My words are breathy, and I feel light-headed from the waves of arousal washing over me.

I quickly walk away from him. *This is too damn much for a thirty-four-year-old virgin. Then again, it may not be enough, considering I'm a thirty-four-year-old virgin.*

As expected, I find Adeline under my bed, seeking refuge in her special hiding place. She's snuggled under a pink quilt, and her red eyes and tear-stained cheeks tug at my heart.

"Hi, squirt. Come here."

She crawls out from her safe haven into my lap. I hold her close and kiss her forehead and wait to see if she'll say something, anything that will tell me where her mind is right now.

"Addie? How do you feel, sweetheart?"

She shakes her head and nuzzles closer to me. She sniffles and holds me tighter, and I'm thinking I should have showed her the photo album Jackson brought with her. I struggle a little to stand without putting her down and make my way down the hall to her bedroom. She lets me set her in the center of her bed, so I kiss her forehead before I go to her closet and pull out the box.

I remove the lid and search through the items until I find what I'm looking for. I climb on the bed and welcome her to sit in my lap again, then open her family photo album. I flip the pages slowly so she can get a good look at all the memories.

I think of how cheated this little girl's life is that her parents were taken from her so soon. Over time, she'll forget the few years of memories she hangs onto now. I try to shake the hopeless thoughts from my mind and direct her attention to a picture of her father and his brother at what looks like their high school graduation. They look so young but still overwhelmingly good-looking. In the photo, Trevor doesn't have his long locks or neatly trimmed goatee, making him unrecognizable as the man waiting in my kitchen.

"Can you tell which one of these men is your father?" I ask.

She shakes her head, and I flip to another photo. In this one, they're clearly two different men. Trevor has more facial hair and more hair on his head. I'm guessing during this time he decided to grow it out for his dreads. I ask the same question.

She's quietly examining the photo, then she points at the man with the close cut and clean-shaven face. "Daddy."

I smile. "Yes, he is your daddy, and this man"—I point—"is your uncle Trevor. Your daddy and Trevor were identical twins. Do you know what that means?"

"They're the same."

"They only look the same. They're very different people. The man in my kitchen is who?"

"My uncle Trevor."

"Yes, and he's been out of the country for some years now, but he'll be caring for you now, which is what your dad wanted."

"What room will he take?"

I frown, not understanding the question.

She knows she stumped me, because she turns to look at me. "Will he sleep with you or in the room me and my friends play in?"

I blush at the thought of Trevor between my sheets but don't cringe at the idea of him sharing my space. Oddly, the thought comforts me. "No, he won't be moving in with me. You'll go with him and live where he lives."

It's her turn to frown. "And where is that? Will I also go out of the country too?"

"I don't know, squirt, but I'm sure you'll love it there."

"I love it here. I like your house. It makes me happy, and it always smells like sugar."

I giggle and give her a tight hug. I don't answer her though, because I don't know what to say. I don't know Trevor's plans for Adeline, but I'll make sure to ask. "Come on, let's go introduce you to your uncle. Are you ready to see him?"

"Yes, but I'm scared. Do you think Daddy can see me through Uncle's eyes? They have the same eyes."

I smile but also feel a sting of sadness. "Let's ask your uncle."

I stand beside her bed and hold out my hand for her to take, but she surprises me by raising her arms for me to pick her up. I smile but feel like crying. Right now, Adeline couldn't care less about being a big girl. She needs to be comforted and reassured that she's safe, and I'm happy that I can give it to her.

We make our way back to the kitchen. I turn the corner and stop short, not believing the sight before me. Trevor's sports jacket has been tossed over the back of one of the barstools. His shirtsleeves are rolled up his forearms and the top two buttons are undone. He's standing at my stove, emptying perfectly fluffy eggs onto a serving plate. On my kitchen table, he has laid out stacks of pancakes—more than we can eat—bacon and sausage. He took out more berries, and they are clean, sliced, and dusted with powdered sugar. He even set the table for three.

"What the hell?" I whisper.

He looks up, and Adeline turns her head to see what has shocked me enough to curse. I quickly kiss her cheek and excuse my language before setting her down at the table.

3

TREVOR

After I signed the papers for the rental house, I googled Peggy's home address, only a couple miles from mine. I called but there was no answer. I left a message that I arrived early and would be stopping by her home because I was close.

When I make my turn, I notice the cottage-style house with large veranda at the end of the road and wonder what type of person Peggy Jordan is. Over the phone, she sounded young and sweet. When we discussed Adeline on these phone calls, she spoke of her with so much compassion and love. Talking to Peggy was the highlight of my day. She makes me feel like there is light at the end of the tunnel. Only my mother could give me that feeling, I'm happy such a person is looking after my niece.

I park my rental car and walk up the front steps, looking down the veranda from left to right. It's decked out with cozy outdoor pillows on white wicker furniture and lush potted greenery. The "Welcome Home" doormat makes me smile, because that was my first impression of her home. I have the strong urge to remove my shoes and socks, strip out of these stuffy clothes, and slip on a pair of loose shorts, shirtless so I can feel the sun on my skin.

A rush of anxious energy floods me, and I knock at the door. At the same time I knock, the house floods with the sound of music and it's clear my knocks weren't heard. I try the bell, hoping it might announce my presence, but no answer. I peek through the window and see two silhouettes through the sheer curtains. The music blares louder.

I walk around and stand in the doorway of her open French doors, and I stop breathing. The entire scene reminds me of my childhood, of happier times before my mom got sick, and brings a tear to my eye. My heart aches to be a part of this picture. I watch my niece bopping her head of messy curls to the music while popping fruit in her mouth and deciding what color to choose from her caddy of a hundred choices. She smiles and it's the same one as my mother's.

She directs her joy at the most beautiful woman I've ever seen. I rest my hand over my heart, trying to decide whether I'm holding it in place or ripping it from my chest and willingly offering it to her.

She's dancing around the kitchen with whitewash cabinets and a sage-green island. I would expect this in the home of a sweet Southern grandmother with fresh homemade treats and pies cooling on the windowsills, but strangely, it seems to fit her perfectly. She's wearing the smallest shorts, but her curvy bottom is completely covered. Her arms and legs are exposed, and what a pair of legs they are. She's slim but carries generous curves in all the right places. Her creamy cinnamon skin makes my mouth water. Her face is clean, and her full natural curls fall effortlessly around her face and past her sexy shoulders.

She's cooking and caring for Adeline, and a picture of her belly round with our baby growing inside her invades my mind. Her feet are bare, and every few steps, she perches up on her tiptoes, as if it's a habit she never grew out of. I don't understand where all these feelings are coming from, but whoever this woman is, she's mine now.

It's real caveman of me to claim another person like a seat on the bus, but I don't give a fuck. I only want to be in her presence and breathe the same air she does. Want her to run her fingers over my back while I worship her body and take care of her. I ache for her to wrap me in her arms and whisper reassuring words that I'm not alone, that I can do right by my niece and make my brother proud of me.

She instructs Adeline to wash her hands, and I close my eyes and allow the familiar sweet voice to wash over me.

I can't take being ignored by her any longer. I want her eyes on me. Want her to acknowledge me. I want Peggy Jordan to welcome me into her space, into her life.

"Something sure smells good."

Startled, she jumps, and grease hits her thigh, burning her skin.

Fuck, that wasn't smart, Trevor.

I hurry to her side and take the wet towel from her hands. I kneel at her feet and grab her thigh, pressing the cool towel to her beautiful skin. Staring up at Peggy, I pray she forgives me for causing her to burn herself, when my niece screams the house down and flees the room. Disgusted with myself for causing so much shit—*talk about first impressions*—I frown, shaking my head.

Peggy calls out for Adeline, then turns her attention back to me, and my spirits brighten some. I hate that Adeline is upset, but there's nothing that could be done about it.

Peggy's one word question about my identity pulls my eyes from her thigh to her face again.

Her skin flushes, and I've fallen in love. It's not lust at first sight because I'm not thinking of fucking her. I'm consumed with my need to be important to her, to share this life with her.

"Trevor Duncan. I presume you're Peggy Jordan."

She frowns, and nervousness tightens my gut. I don't know what she's thinking, then she hesitates her words. I decide to try being charming, fearing she'll kick my ass out her house. Peggy presses her sexy lips together in a thin line and her beautiful face shows annoyance at me.

"So you're not pleased?" I smile, hoping to change the look on her face.

She lifts her left eyebrow and her eyes shoot daggers my way.

"I called but there was no answer. I left a message saying I was close and would drop by. Also I did ring the bell and knocked. I heard the music—"

"And you decide to break and enter instead?" Peggy attempts another go at moving my hand, but I must make sure she's okay.

I smile. "Breaking and entering? Not quite."

"You startled me! I burned my leg, and let's not forget you frightened the hell out of your niece."

I feel like a fucking joke for thinking I could have Peggy, that she would be mine, that I would have the privilege to share her life. I offer an apology, because what else can I say? I want to beg her to tell me what I need to do to make her happy.

When I remove the towel, a small red dot marks her beautiful skin, and I figure I can start with a show of remorse. Besides, I want a small taste of her. After moistening my lips, I press an apologetic kiss to the burn to aid in easing her pain. Peggy gasps her surprise, and I also get a good whiff of her arousal. I stand before I can nestle my face between her thighs and attempt to get lost in her sweet scent.

Peggy's eyes roam down my body, and I shiver under her visual caress. I don't take my eyes off her face, wanting to read her expressions or guess what she's thinking. Is something there that I missed before? But she steps away from me, and I don't like that she's putting distance between us. I want her to know that I know that I pique her interest.

She's breathing erratically and her pebbled nipples are straining against the fabric of her top, begging for my attention. Peggy turns and gives me her back. She must realize that her body is betraying her. I move closer, refusing to let her pull away from me. She mentions Adeline hiding in her bedroom, and I offer to help. *Why the hell not ask? The worse that could happen, she says—*

"No!" Peggy half screams with her hands raised.

I step right into them, desperate for her touch. As soon as her warm palms rest on my abs, my muscles jump, reacting to the longing that shoots through me. Peggy refuses to look at me. I'm pissed but relieved, because she does need to tend to Adeline, and if I see her desire for me as clearly as I can smell it, I won't be able to control myself. However, I hate that Peggy's hiding from me.

She leaves the kitchen, and I follow her to the entryway, where she walks up the stairs and turns to the right before disappearing. I smile because now I know that her bedroom is on the right side of the house.

I shake my head at the ridiculousness of my behavior. I feel like a crazy, obsessed creep. I've never in my life felt the way I did when I first laid eyes on Peggy Jordan. Fuck that, if I'm being honest, I felt something when I first heard her sweet voice on the phone.

My eyes scan the kitchen again. The Southern charm displayed in her taste gives me another fact about Ms. Jordan—she's as sweet as she smells. She's traditional and old-fashioned, and the use of lace and tapestry in her décor possibly means Peggy's a romantic. I poke around, exploring a little more—at least the rooms that are open to the kitchen.

Her family room is decorated just like the kitchen, and I wouldn't be surprised if the entire home is the same. She uses a vast number of pillows. That suggests Peggy may be a loner, or just alone a lot, because she wants to cuddle something everywhere she sits. The pillows could also mean she's single. *God, please let this woman be unattached.* I'm not a religious person but I believe in God, and the last time I remember praying, even a little, was when my mom was battling cancer.

I look at her collection of framed photos on the built-in selves on either side of her fireplace. She seems to have little family, but they're all important to her. An obituary of a couple, their wedding bands, two long-stem dried roses, and a rosary are in a shadow box over the fireplace.

Upon closer inspection, I see the names *Jamison and Patricia Jordan*. I assume they are Peggy's parents. According to the date, I was in my mid-twenties when they passed, and I wonder how old

Peggy was and how she dealt with the loss of both parents at once. That leads me to wonder if that's why Jackson chose Peggy—his daughter's college roommate—to care for Adeline, because she could relate to my niece's loss.

I thank God again for placing Adeline with Peggy. My eyes land on a framed picture of Peggy and Adeline, both in pink swimsuits and white sunglasses, standing in front of a large spray of water. Their hair is drenched and sticking to their skin. That must have been when she took Adeline to the water park.

I see one of Adeline with dirty hands, palming a large tomato, and her smile is so beautiful my chest tightens. Next to that is one of Adeline with two other kids who look to be her age. They're huddled in front of a wooden playground, their arms over each other's shoulders. My love for Peggy Jordan deepens because of her beautiful heart and how open she is to loving other people.

I hear footsteps and peek around the corner, looking up to the second-level landing. Peggy is carrying Adeline to the other side of the house. When they disappear, I make my way back to her kitchen, promising myself that I'll make a place for myself on her family wall. *Maybe the first picture will be our wedding photo.* I smile at the thought and decide that the first thing I'm going to do is feed my woman and my niece. Peggy was cooking for Adeline when I first arrived, so I'll continue what she started.

I remove my jacket and roll up my sleeves. First, I open all her cabinets and familiarize myself with the layout of her kitchen. Peggy's organized, and her well-thought-out kitchen makes for an easy work flow. I pull out the ingredients I need to make more pancake batter, and the first thing I notice in her fridge is her taste for imported beer. I'm convinced Peggy Jordan was created for me. I pull open the meat drawer and grab more bacon and breakfast sausage.

I open the dishwasher and notice it's empty, so I fill her country sink with hot water. As I finish cooking breakfast, I submerge the dishes in the hot water before placing them in the dishwasher. When I'm done, the table is set with more food than the three of us can eat—a hard habit to break after living and working the past fourteen years with large groups.

"What the hell?"

The words are whispered but loud enough that I turn and see Peggy holding Adeline, an expression of shock on her beautiful face. Peggy carries Adeline to the table and stares before sitting her on the middle chair. I walk over to them and extend my hand to Adeline, wanting to make things right with her by introducing myself.

"Hi, Adeline. I'm your uncle Trevor. It's a great pleasure to finally meet you."

Adeline places her small hand on my large palm and I close my fingers, giving her a gentle squeeze. She's staring at me with eyes full of wonder.

"I made you and Peggy a pancake breakfast. I hear pancakes are your favorite."

She nods and adds, "With lots of honey and berries too."

I nod and release her little hand from mine and step aside. I walk over and grab the plate. I stand behind Peggy, wanting to smell her, but all I smell is breakfast. I move closer to her and place the plate of eggs on the table.

She turns her head and looks up at me. I want another taste of her so badly. Her face is so close and my eyes move to her lips, and I notice she does the same to mine.

The tip of her tongue makes a quick pass over her lips, and I have to close my eyes and pray for control, but then I hear her whisper, "Trevor."

I open my eyes to see the warm whisky color of her irises, and they're pulling me in, calling, pleading. She appears taller, her lips closer to mine, and I remember her tippy-toe habit.

Not thinking of Adeline sitting mere inches from us, I lean in, wanting to satisfy my desire for Peggy and taste her sweet lips. At least that's what I thought was going to happen. She jerks her head away from my in-coming mouth, as if suddenly realizing what was happening between us.

"Thank you," she whispers instead, and her warm breath tickles my neck.

"You're welcome Peggy, " I say softly. "Now, let's eat."

Adeline cheers, bouncing in her chair and pointing at the fruit I sliced.

Peggy goes to serve Adeline, but I wrap my hand around hers. "I'll get it. Please sit. You've been caring for Adeline these past months."

Without putting up a fuss, Peggy takes her seat, and her smile looks as sweet and innocent as Adeline's. The urge to hold her is so strong, I have to tighten my grip on the serving spoon. I proceed to plating food for Peggy and Adeline. While they're enjoying, I clean up the rest of the mess I made while cooking.

"Peggy."

It's a man's voice, and my heart leaps into my throat before I even look up at the man standing in the doorway, a box in his hands. He's my height but slimmer, and he looks as though he's from around here. A good ol' Southern boy with his buzz cut, jeans, V-neck T-shirt, and cowboy boots. His tan skin clearly comes from excessive sun exposure, however, it enhances the hazel-green of his eyes.

Adeline jumps off her chair and runs to him. "William!"

She gives him the same smile—my mother's smile—that she gives Peggy, and I instantly hate him. I hate that she doesn't know me, her only family.

He calls her squirt before picking her up and walking her back to the table. He's still holding the box.

"They did it again, I see." Peggy stands from her seat, next to him, and takes the box from his hands.

"Yep, UPS just left it on my doorstep an hour ago."

"Well, thank you for bringing it right over." She gives him a smile she has yet to give me.

Seeing them together, him holding Adeline and Peggy by his side, I fume. *Who the fuck is this guy? I haven't seen one fucking photo of his ugly mug anywhere on her family wall. Unless she has it on the* nightstand—what the fuck! She better not, that's where our picture belongs. But you never asked her if she was seeing anyone, jackass. I never got the fucking chance to. Well, now is as good a time as any. I put the last of the pots in the dishwasher and try to quiet the conversation I'm having in my head.

"Is that my Minnie Mouse lamp?" Adeline squirms in his arms, and he stands her on the chair.

"I sure hope so, squirt," Peggy says.

"Uncle Trevor, come look. Peggy got me a Minnie Mouse lamp!"

Hearing her say my name, inviting me to join in her joy and excitement, lowers my anger to a simmer. I walk around the island, grab my jacket on the way, and drape it over Peggy's shoulders. "That's wonderful, Adeline."

Peggy offers me a small smirk before returning to her task of opening the box. I'm happy she didn't put up a fuss about the jacket, because I would have tossed her over my shoulder and marched up to her bedroom, demanding she cover up what's mine.

"William Perkins," Mr. Good ol' Boy announces, holding out a hand to me.

"Oh my, where are my manners? Trevor, William is my next-door neighbor and good friend. William, Trevor Duncan is Adeline's uncle. He's here for her." She shrugs her delicate shoulders under my oversized jacket.

"I'm here to stay," I say, correcting her statement. I figure I should start warming her up to the idea of having me around. The only way I'm going anywhere without her is my grave.

I shake his hand and note that she never said he was a boyfriend, just a good friend. I also notice that his eyes haven't left her.

"Would you like to stay for breakfast, William? Trevor cooked, and as you see, he made more than we can eat."

I don't say a word because I know whatever will come from my mouth will sound more like, "Get the hell out." Fuck, I'll eat myself in a coma just to not share this meal with Mr. Good ol' Boy.

He pulls his eyes from Peggy and looks at me before he answers. "I can't, I have some business in town. But we're still on for Thursday night?" He meets my stare.

My body tenses, and I growl through my thoughts, *Hell the fuck no.*

Peggy looks at me as if she heard my thoughts. I see her blush before she turns back to the neighbor-slash-good friend. "I'll let you know."

4
PEGGY

"How old was Clarisse when you became her guardian?" Trevor asks. We're sitting on my back patio, watching Adeline play, and I just told him about my younger sister, whom I partially raised.

"Clarisse was thirteen. Adeline's younger than she was, but I understand her pain and know how important it is to be patient through the grieving process."

He nods his understanding.

"That must be the reason Jackson chose you to take Adeline."

"That could be true. He…" Taking me by surprise, Trevor holds my left hand in his right one and intertwine our fingers. I stare at him then glance down at our hands. The move is a subtle show of affection, but I'm equally perturbed and completely turned on, the same when he kissed my burned thigh.

"Is this ok?" He gestures to our hands. I'm guessing he didn't miss my reaction.

"If I say no, will you release your hold on my fingers?"

"No."

His lips spread across his gorgeous face, and I believe I'm in trouble. I don't address it any further. What's the point when I love how my hand in his feels.

"He knows the experience I have personally and also professionally. Until recently, I was a social worker. Two weeks before Jack called me regarding Adeline, I quit that job, wanting to focus on a dream I've always held close to my heart."

"Which is?" He asks.

"Homemade, home grown fruits and vegetables. I want my own stand at the farmers market, to supply grocery stores with healthy, home grown foods." I point to the plot of land I garden on, and my greenhouse. Trevor turns my way and smiles at me.

It's a smile I hadn't seen. His expression looks as if I just gave him the best gift he didn't know he wanted. He gives my hand a firm yet gentle squeeze before passing his thumb over my knuckles.

All morning, we've talked about his travels and the many places he has lived over the last fourteen years. He amazed Adeline with tales of wild animals in the jungle and a time he rode a camel in the desert. Since that story, she's been giving him a dreamy gaze every time he talks to her.

I believe I'm no better because, every question Trevor asks, I vomit out the truth. In the span of four hours, I've told him more about my life than I've told my own sister. Trevor knows how scared I was after realizing I had to raise my younger sister, and some of the mistakes I made along the way. Trevor knows I became an adult in the environment of a professional model. From eleven to twenty-one, I was one of the most sought-after high fashion, print models in the industry. What he doesn't know is why I quit, and that's only because he hasn't asked me directly.

"Tell me about your tiptoe habit."

He completely takes me by surprise again. I frown, confused. "What habit?"

Trevor's smile widens, and I wonder if he's pulling my leg.

"Is this some joke? I don't tiptoe," I say.

He releases my hand and stands. He straddles the bottom my

lounge chair, grabs my ankles, and brings my feet up to his line of sight. I giggle and squirm, trying to free my bare feet from his grasp because I'm extremely ticklish.

"What in the hell are you doing?" I'm giggling like an idiot. "Do you make a habit of grabbing on women? I don't know what you're talking about."

"When you're moving all these beautiful curves around, you occasionally arch your feet and twirl on tiptoe. I'll give you one last chance, Ms. Jordan, to tell the truth."

Trevor's gaze meets mine, and I feel dizzy. His stare is so intense, I can feel his touch all over my body, not just on my feet. He places my feet on either side of his trouser-clad thighs. I'm still in my white shorts and tank top, and now my legs are spread wide and my feet dangling.

"The truth," Trevor demands before tickling my bare foot.

I laugh and squirm, trying to shield my foot from his ruthless attack, but he's not giving up. I try pushing against his hold on my ankle, but he's not budging. Finally, I can't take his sweet torture and give in. "Fine, fine! Just give me a minute."

He releases my foot and allows me to collect myself. I consider his account of my so-called habit and decide Trevor may be right, that I do have that habit.

"I don't know... I mean, I'm not aware of it, so I can only assume it's left over from my modeling days. Always in heels, it became my norm and I guess a habit. But seriously, I was never aware of it."

His hazel eyes soften as he considers my explanation. He leans forward, a gentle smile on his gorgeous face. My eyes flutter closed at the feel of his warm breath on my left ear.

"Thank you," he whispers, and I can hear he's smiling.

"For what?" I pull back to clear my head. His proximity teases my body's need for physical contact. My sexual desires have been dormant and since laying eyes on Trevor, desire is stirring inside me and a gush of warmth pools at my center, drenching my panties.

"For taking in Adeline, for sharing so much about your life with me, for not removing my jacket earlier."

I fall back in my lounge chair when a burst of laughter leaves me. Draping my barely-dressed body with his jacket made me feel protected by Trevor. I wore the damn thing all through breakfast like an idiot because it smelled like him. He smells like summers in the south, like home.

I sit up and scoot my bottom, bringing me closer to him. "You're welcome."

"Damn, woman, you smell delicious." He groans.

My face warms and I avert my gaze, not knowing what to say. Trevor slides back from me and plants his sexy ass back in the Adirondack chair next to mine. He grabs my hand again and rubs my knuckles with his thumb. I go with it because it feels so natural for us to be like this.

"What are your plans?" I ask. I understand it's important to know before I get pulled into Trevor more than I already have been. It already happened with Adeline.

He takes a deep breath and exhales as though I asked him to bring an end to world hunger. I sense a change in him, a tension that wasn't there before. He's staring at Addie playing in my backyard, but his focus is so far away.

Concern creeps in my gut. I know what he's feeling, with just finding out about his brother and having to plan a life for a five-year-old niece he met mere hours ago. I was in Trevor's shoes once. I can't explain the magnitude of strength it takes for a person to willingly take on such a task. I gently squeeze his hand and he smiles, but never looks at me.

"Well, we have an appointment with social services in two days. So I have two days to get my life lined up. I have a shit-load of red tape to cut through with my brother's estate, on top of taking responsibility of my family's casino in Vegas. I rented a small two-bedroom house near here, at least for the next couple of months while I work on a more permanent place."

I frown and turn to watch Adeline hard at play. Jackson told me about the Duncan family own a large casino and hotel. I guess I have a couple of months before they head to Vegas.

The pain in my heart is so intense, I grab at my chest. The thought of Adeline leaving me is a reality I'm not ready for, and as insane as it may sound, the pain of being away from Trevor goes bone deep. My thoughts run through the day's events, including Trevor nursing my burned thigh, breakfast, and how quickly he and Adeline hit it off. The awe and admiration in her eyes when she looks so lovingly at him.

"She has her room here and all of her things—her Minnie Mouse lamp and all." I smile and look his way. He smiles, and I know he's thinking of how bossy Adeline was, directing him to place her lamp in just the right spot in her room. I enjoyed seeing this big man handle her delicate trinkets. "I have a spare room. If you want, it's yours." *Not sure why I offered for him to move in, but in an insane way it feels right, and then I won't have to give up Adeline too soon.*

Trevor turns to me with a thoughtful expression on his face. I'm thinking it's gratitude and he's going to accept my crazy out of character, out of the blue invitation. So I thought.

"Peggy, that's very generous of you, but I can't do that. You've had Adeline interrupting your life for two months. I can't allow you to put up with a strange man in your home, too."

Only God knows how much I want him to stay with me, but Trevor is right. Neither him or Adeline belong to me and I have to let go. I shift my hand in his and grab his hand in mine. With my smaller hand around his bigger one, I rub my thumb over his knuckles.

"Trevor, you're no strange man. You're special to Adeline and…you're special to m—"

Dear God, I almost said it. I almost admitted to my crazy, out-of-control feelings.

He didn't respond to my almost-confession. He only smiles knowingly and lifts our linked hands to his lips and kisses the tips of my fingers that grip his.

He doesn't understand the magnitude my statement has on my life. Because of past trauma I've experienced with men—well, one man in particular—Trevor is the only man I've felt safe with in years. The only other person who'd ever been able to get me to talk and explore my feelings and emotions was my mother. She traveled with me until I was nineteen, then she returned to Savannah. During our time together she was my safe haven, my place to go when I was afraid and unsure of myself. The calm that washes over me when Trevor is near me feels familiar but very new. It's become very addicting, very quickly.

I check the time, and it's nearing four o'clock. I call for Adeline to come in a wash up so we can start dinner.

"How about I take us out for dinner?" Trevor offers.

"But what about pizza and a movie night?" Adeline chimes in, her sweaty face is upturned to Trevor. Her cheeks are flush from the exertion of her single player soccer match.

"Then pizza and a movie you'll have." He scoops her up and rushes her into the house, her laughter trailing behind them.

Trevor tries to make up for disrupting our usual Saturday tradition by treating us to a drive-thru movie and take-out pizza. It isn't the same experience as Adeline and I preparing the dough, slipping on our rubber boots, and heading to the garden with baskets in hand, picking our selected toppings. But nevertheless it's an amazing night.

While camping out in the back of my SUV eating the pizza, Trevor and I decide to explain to Adeline that after their meeting with social services, she'll go to live with Trevor. At the end of the explanation, we're faced with watery eyes and a few negotiation sessions, but I tell her she can come visit me whenever she desires, and that my door is always open to her and her uncle.

"Will I still have my play date next weekend with Riley and FJ?"

"Of course you will, squirt," I answer.

"The house I'm renting for us to live in is only a few fast

minutes from Peggy," Trevor adds. "We won't be far from her at all."

Adeline looks down at her slice of pizza and proceeds to eat all the meat before she nods and concedes to the terms. Adeline's acceptance of her life moving forward makes me want to scream and cry. I'm talking full blown, face down on the ground, kicking tantrum. This shouldn't be that hard. I've placed kids and walked away hundreds and hundreds of times, but a piece of my heart will break off when Adeline leaves me.

She dozes off before the movie is over—like always, with a full tummy. She sleeps curled in my lap while Trevor drives at a snail's pace home because she and I are sharing a seat belt. I almost doze off myself, but I'm not ready for the night to end with Trevor.

"If you get her out the car and take her upstairs, I'll tuck her in," I say.

"Yes, ma'am." He unfolds his tall frame from my SUV and does as I ask, leaving me to settle Adeline in bed. I toss her clothes in the hamper and slip on her night dress, all without waking her from her deep sleep.

When I make my way downstairs, Trevor is standing in the entry with his jacket folded over a forearm and his hands stuff in his pant pockets. He's so distracting I almost ignore the calming creaks of the floorboards.

"I can make us coffee. If you like?" My bare feet hits the last step. I can tell he's trying to leave, but I want him to know he can stay longer—if he chooses.

"Nah, I should get going. It's late, and don't think I didn't notice you dozing off on the ride back."

"Only because you were driving Miss Daisy." I fist my hips and squint my eyes at him.

He chuckles and the smooth, seductive sound hits me like an invisible force and pulls me toward him. I obey my body's order and take a few step to close the distance between us. I'm standing mere inches from his body. His heat envelops me in a cocoon of lust, and my inside begins to shake. I feel drunk and willing.

Trevor has yet to touch me, but his gaze is enough to bring forth a moan from my body. I'm unaware of how long we stand in my entry eye-fucking one another, but I'm growing impatient. He must sense my feelings because he lifts his left hand and passes the pad of his thumb over my bottom lip.

"Shhh."

He palms my right cheek with his fingers splayed and caresses the side of my face and neck at once. I rub into his palms like an attention seeking kitten and damn near purr like one too.

"Trevor…"

"Good night, Peggy," he whispers. He backs away, turns, and walks out. For the second time in my adult life, I feel a screaming, crying, face down on the ground, kicking tantrum brewing in the pit of my stomach, and I don't care what it says about me when it comes to Trevor.

∽

NEARLY A WEEK ago Trevor caused the worst sleepless night of my entire life. I can still feel his touch on my face. So far, Adeline hasn't missed spending a day with me. Trevor hasn't either.

During one of our nightly phone conversations, he offered to set up a sprinkler system for me, and these last few days he's generously been hard at work installing the pipe. I asked for a price for parts and labor, but he has yet to give a number and has just about completed the job. I'm standing in the middle of Adeline's art room—I mean, my sunroom—watching Trevor adjust the sprinkler heads outside.

Adeline is helping the best she can—which means very little. Right now she's unsuccessfully trying to dodge the sprays of water. Her hair and jean overalls are soaked.

I haven't changed her room and I don't believe I will. Call it wishful thinking, but she may ask to sleep over. I walk out onto the side veranda and watch Trevor strut across my property. His dreads are pulled up into a top knot. His damp white t-shirt clings to his hard flesh from the spray of water and sweat. The way his muscles expand, stretching the fabric of his clothes, has my skin sizzling like I'm experiencing menopausal hot flashes. I have to catch my breath and possibly change my panties.

"How's it coming along?" I ask while I help Adeline remove her rubber boots. I instruct her to run up and change out of her wet clothes and after, her snack is at the island. Trevor's using the garden hose to wash away the grime from his hands and wet his face. I lean over the railing and hand him a glass of ice tea.

"I'm done," he says with a bright, satisfied smile on his face. "Thank you." He takes the glass and drains it empty of the cold, sweet, homemade tea.

"I guess I should expect to receive a bill." I give him a pointed look and raise an eyebrow.

He chuckles and hands me the empty glass. Then shakes his head and walks around the front of the house.

"What in the hell is so funny!" I set the glass on the railing and walk around the veranda to the front of the house. "Trevor!"

He stops walking with one heavy boot hitting the front steps. I'm blocking his way with my hands on my hips. From where I stand, I'm equal to his height, glaring at him eye to eye, nose to nose, lips to lips. I break eye contact a minute when my sights go to his sexy lips set in a smooth smile.

"You. You're what's funny."

"I'll give you five seconds to explain, Mr. Duncan."

His smile returns and I'm getting more and more frustrated with him. I feel my face heat and I begin to count.

"One... Two... Three—" Trevor swoops me up into his arms and flips my body over his shoulder like I'm light as a feather. "Trevor! Put me down!"

I'm happy I have on shorts. He walks up the stairs and into my house as if he's taking a morning stroll. I'm annoyed on top of sexually frustrated, and the feel of his hard body under me and the occasional puff of his warm breath on my thigh is driving me crazy. I tighten my core to keep from moaning but that makes my achy center throb.

"Trevor, please put me down." My plea sounds weak.

"In due time. What I have to say may compel you to lash out at me. Holding onto you will ensure I make it through this unscathed."

"Maybe. You do have to put me down some time."

"I could hold you forever, woman."

Well shit. There goes my temper, and I give in, slumping over his shoulder. "Say your peace, Trevor."

"There's no bill. This one is on me."

"Like hell!" I squirm and Trevor lifts me from his shoulder. As soon as my feet touches the hardwood floor, I push away from him. "Trevor…"

"Before you chastise me, can I first say it's my pleasure to do this for you."

"Chastise!" My hands find their place back on my hips. "Voicing my opinion about any matter concerning… Well… anything, Mr. Duncan, never will be me chastising, nagging, emotional, sensitive, or even is it that time of the month. If I don't agree with you or any man, and I choose to say how I feel, that doesn't make me problematic. It makes me smart enough to handle my own fucking affairs!"

I understand the cost of the materials equals pennies considering how many millions or even billions Trevor is worth, but I'm not struggling financially. The house was paid off before my parents died, and ten years stacking my modeling money on top of nine years with a steady salary as a social worker, I live a very comfortable life.

I quickly glance up at the landing, making sure Adeline didn't witness my outburst. When I don't see her, I lower my voice and try to compromise. "Thank you so much for wanting to install a sprinkler system for me because it pleases you to be a nice person. Thank you for the labor. How much do I owe for the materials?"

He clears his throat. "A few hundred bucks."

"Great, I'll write you a check."

"Yes, ma'am." He nods and smiles his bright, satisfied smile at me.

∽

I'M PASSING the broom in my kitchen, attempting to clean up as much of the flour from my homemade pie crusts and pizza dough as I can. It's another pizza and movie Saturday, and Trevor hasn't come over with Adeline yet. I check the time again and it's almost noon.

Clarisse's nanny will be here around two with the twins for the play date. Adeline has been so excited for this day all week. Before they took off last night, she promised to go to sleep fast so morning could come quicker.

When Trevor wasn't at my door bright and early with Adeline and a cup of Starbucks coffee, my first thought was to text him. Instead of, *Are you still coming?* I texted, *Missing my morning cup of Joe.* I have yet to receive a reply.

After putting away the broom and dust pan, I walk over to the work desk in the corner of my kitchen and grab my cell from the charger. I pull up Trevor's number, ready to call, when a hard knock to the front door startles me. I power walk to the front entry and open the heavy wood door. Adeline rushes in and hugs my legs so tight, as if she didn't just leave me last night. Her hair is all over her head, and she's wearing rubber boots with her night clothes.

She looks a hot mess. I hold her face in my hands and lift it so I can see her expression. "Is everything okay?"

"No."

"What happened?" I ask.

"Water pipe broke sometime in the middle of the night." He's holding a cup of Starbucks coffee. I'm guessing he saw my text. I smile and take the cup. "We woke to water everywhere this morning. I'm thankful it only reached the top of the baseboards. Hate to think what could have happened if it touched the wall plugs in that old house."

My blood runs cold and I feel lightheaded at the thought. I recall when I first laid eyes on that old house, I questioned Trevor's logic. Here he is with enough money to purchase three of my houses with no discomfort, and he settles on renting a small, old house.

"'It's my first home. We don't need much, and it's temporary,'" he had told me, and I realized Trevor was no typical rich asshole.

I hold Adeline tight and move from in front of the door. I'm squeezing her, repeatedly kissing her cheek, grateful to see her face. When I think I've composed myself, I pull back and ask her to head upstairs so she can cleanup and dress before her play date. She runs up the stairs to her room, and I rush into Trevor's waiting arms.

I'm holding him a little awkward because of my coffee cup, but Trevor has me completely engulfed in a strong embrace. "What are you going to do?"

He takes a breath before answering. "I reserved a room at a hotel in town."

"Why?" I give him a confused look. "You know you can stay here. Adeline has gone through so many changes. Her room is familiar, and we have a routine." I smile before adding, "The two of you are here over ninety percent of the day anyway."

Trevor gives me a smile and I pray he agrees. I make one more attempt at getting my way, but this next statement is equally as true as the last. "I'm so happy you and Adeline are safe. To even give the smallest of my energy to the thoughts of what could have happened... I want to lock you both away so you're safe forever. Right now I need you to say yes, Trevor."

∽

I'M PLACING fresh linens on the bed in my downstairs guest bedroom while Trevor retrieves his luggage from his car. I've gone so far as to cut flowers from my rose garden out back and place a few bouquets in his room. I check the ensuite and placed clean white towels on the shelves.

"Peggy! He's coming! He's coming!" Adeline yells loud enough to wake the dead.

I run from the bathroom and hit a wall of solid muscle. Trevor wraps me into an embrace to steady me while I attempt to catch my breath.

"Why the rush?" he asks, smiling at me, and I feel small. His broad physique dwarfs my slightly slender, five-foot-eight frame.

"I-I was getting your room ready." I struggle to catch my breath because he's still holding me close, and his hard body has mine shaking. "No one has used this room in a while. I don't have many overnight visitors. When my niece and nephew sleep over, they camp out in the upstairs playroom."

"I told you he was coming." Adeline peeks from around Trevor, sporting a huge grin.

"I heard you, squirt, but more notice would've been great."

Trevor has a tight hold on me, and I'm dizzy with need from being wrapped into him. His hard body pressed against mine has me wondering if he's hard all over, and my face flushes. I rest my forehead on his chest, not wanting him to see my reaction, but I was too late. His warm hands palm my face, and his thumbs pass over my cheeks. I hold my breath, waiting for the comment I'm sure will embarrass me further, but he shows mercy and releases me.

Adeline giggles, and I step back before walking past him to the bathroom door. "Well, I'll let you get to it. I put fresh towels out, and there are extra blankets in the armoire if you get cold at night." I point at the large antique piece in the corner of the room. "I try to keep the house comfortable in the evenings."

He nods and tosses his large duffle bag on the luggage stand at the foot of the bed. "You want to help me unpack a few things, Adeline?"

As I leave the bedroom, she cheers her approval. "I'll start dinner," I say.

"If you give me twenty minutes, I'll help."

His voice makes me smile, and my cheeks heat once again. I've never had someone wait on me before. Trevor was great at hosting his first play date. He put together the best grilled cheese sandwiches I've ever had. Adeline, the twins, and I were full after having two sandwiches each. I don't think any of us ate any of the tomato and cucumber salad that's now wrapped up and stored in the fridge for another time. He even gave me a shoulder and back rub after I insisted on loading the dishes since he cooked.

I could get use to this. I could even find myself in love. The thought stops me on my way to the stairs. *Maybe I already am.*

I make my way to my bedroom where I use the twenty minutes he asked for to call my sister. It's been a while since her nanny left with the twins, so I'm sure she's gotten wind of my house guest. I need to keep her at bay until I'm ready to talk about Trevor. For most of our conversation, I allow her to talk about her and her husband reuniting after a major bump in the road in their marriage. Then she asks if I'm ready to meet Adeline's uncle, and I'm surprised. I expected my niece, Riley, would have run into their house with trumpets blaring about the huge handsome man at Aunt Peggy's house. I can only assume the nanny is still out with them.

"I would have been ready if he hadn't arrived early."

"What are you talking about? He's already in the States?"

"Yes, he showed up at my place."

"Unannounced?"

"Can you believe the audacity?" I try to seem pissed. "He claims to have so much red tape to cut through from being gone for so long. Adeline's staying here with me still though."

"Did he ask you to hang on to her?"

"No, but he didn't have to. I love Adeline, and I'm really going to miss her. I love that we have more time together. I would prefer she stay with me period, but Mr. Trevor Duncan has rights. I can't just claim her as mine!"

"You've lost me."

Shit, I lost myself. That's the problem—I've completely lost all sense of reason. I'm rambling and not sure what to say, but until I understand what is happening to me around this man, I have to keep my family none the wiser. Because the fact is, I cannot stomach the thought of him away from me. I'm all over the place. I want to toss my hands up and confide in Clarisse that I want to lose myself in Trevor. I want to tell her the thoughts that have been invading my mind, but to do that, I would have to confess to her that her thirty-four-year-old sister is still a virgin. No one knows that I haven't given myself to a man.

Then I'll have to explain why I'm still untouched, and that's a confession I never want to share with my sister. After that rich, over-privileged asshole slapped my face so hard I temporarily lost sight as he ripped away my clothes, ready to take what he figured was his right—that is, before my friend Jess walked in and tasered him—I've never found a man worthy of my trust or my time.

But the way Trevor rushed to my aid after startling me the morning we first met, the gentle way he handles me, I know—I can't explain how, but I do—Trevor Duncan would never hurt me. His presence calms and soothes what's broken inside me. He makes me want to surrender the hopelessness I've allowed to weigh me down, and I've spent only a week with him.

When my sister ends the call, I'm thankful. I need more time to figure out these feelings before I open an assortment of new problems I'm not ready to deal with. I rush downstairs to the kitchen where I know Trevor is waiting for me. I'm past his promised twenty minutes. Even in my haste, I still find joy in that creaky floorboard at the bottom of the stairs, and I smile.

"I love that," Trevor says when I enter the kitchen.

I assume he's talking about Adeline's drawing, so I peek over her shoulder.

"I mean your smile," he says.

I smile wider, loving how it feels. I can't remember the last time I smiled with every fiber of my existence. He smiles with me. The soft hazel of his eyes warms my skin, and a cozy feeling blankets me. "Sorry I'm late, I took a call from my sister."

"No need to apologize. Adeline has drawn me some amazing pictures while we wait." He holds up two pictures, one a large heart, which she recently learned to draw perfectly. The second is one of her, Riley, and FJ.

"How does this Saturday night tradition work?" Trevor asks.

"It's the best." Adeline answers.

"Saturday's pizza and a movie plays out with Adeline and I eating in the family room around the coffee table watching a movie. Because Adeline loves fruit, I always bake a homemade pie, and tonight it's blueberry. We share the pie right out of the pie dish with vanilla bean ice cream and lots of whipped topping. I want to start on the pie so it can cool while I work on the pizza fixings and roll the dough I prepared earlier." I walk to oven and pre-heat it, then go for my pie crest, when Adeline announces that her art project is complete.

She holds up the paper. "See, I like it. I think it's my best project yet!"

"Well, let's take a look at this best project." Trevor moves around the island and stands to the right of Adeline.

I'm standing to her left. We both lean over her shoulder, checking out her drawing of four figures around a rose garden. I lean in farther, and tears pool in my eyes when I turn to her and she's wearing a warm smile, her eyes bright and beautiful.

I nod. "Yes, squirt, I agree, this is a really good project. I think the picture is so beautiful you should present it to your uncle Trevor. He's never had the privilege of hearing you explain your work."

"Great!" She hops off the barstool. "Follow me, Uncle Trevor."

She waves him over, and he follows her to the sunroom off the kitchen, where more arts and crafts clutter the space. When Adeline came to stay with me, in the beginning we spent most of our days in there. What Adeline couldn't or didn't want to tell me, she spoke through her art projects. I believe this will be the best way for Trevor to really get to know his niece and, more likely than not, his brother too. Adeline walks over to the small easel and clamps her paper at the sides. Trevor stands with his arms crossed.

"Okay, Uncle Trevor, this is Peggy's flower garden. You see all the roses?" She points at the colorful swirls atop long stems. He nods, and she continues. "This is me, and I'm standing next to Peggy, and this is you." She points at the tall figure with long rope-like strings on top of its head. I smile at his thoughtful expression. "Now this is the best part. Are you ready for it, Uncle Trevor?"

"I'm ready, Adeline."

"This is Daddy. See, he's in the sky with wings. He's smiling because you're here with me and with Peggy too. You and Daddy have the same smile." She points out. "I told you it was the best part."

With her big smile, bright eyes, and the sun setting behind her, casting a light over her wild curls, she looks like the angel. I look at Trevor, who has yet to say a word, and the expression on his face stops my heart and sends a sharp pain through me. His raw emotions are on full display, front and center.

He scoops up Adeline, and she wraps her little arms around his neck and squeezes him tightly. She's still smiling, her eyes closed, and I know she's happy that he seems to love her picture, but I know he's hurting for her loss as well as his own. I recall the day he contacted me, the same day he found out about the accident, and I remember the pain I heard in his voice when he asked how Adeline was doing. I don't know a whole hell of a lot about Trevor, but what I do know is that he loves this little girl and regrets the years away from his brother.

I move quietly from the room. I want to be there to comfort him and marvel in the sweet innocence of Adeline's view of the tragedy that brought them together, but I know they need this time alone. Adeline needs to know she can lean on her uncle and he'll be there for her, and Trevor needs the opportunity to absorb the love that Addie gives so freely, the same love that she hooked me with.

Back In the kitchen, I start on dinner.

I turn my sound system to Pandora and select the station inspired by artist Kevin Garrett, one of my favorites for when I'm cooking or cleaning. I close my eyes and relax, swaying my hips to the soulful sound of Parson James's "Waiting Game." From the drawer in front of me, the one that holds all the useless crap I pull from my purse every couple of months, I grab a hair tie. I flip my head forward and pull my curls atop my head, gathering them securely in a pineapple. Then I wash my hands and get to work.

∽

WHEN I PULL the pie from the oven and place it on the cooling rack, I hear Adeline's laughter over my music. It's the fourth or fifth time I've heard that sweet sound, and I know she's going to be okay. Life for her here on out may not be the normal she's used to, but it will be normal enough.

I wonder what they're doing and find myself yearning to be a part of their fun, to be a part of their lives. I want to burst out of these walls that I've made my prison. I want a piece of heaven for myself. I want it with Adeline and Trevor, but the idea is foolish and I shoo it away with the flick of my hand. I'm left fighting a sadness that consumes me. I take a deep breath, brushing a tear from my lashes. I'll push forward as always, so I get back to chopping the rest of the veggies for the pizzas.

Warm, strong hands squeeze my shoulders the same way he did earlier. Trevor starts kneading my tight muscles, working out the tension I was unaware of. I still the knife over the bell pepper and close my eyes, releasing a moan.

"That feels amazing," I say.

He continues to work out the knots in my shoulders, occasionally sliding his thumbs up my neck like before. The way he sees to my comfort melts me and makes me want to cry. The thought enters my mind to shoo him away and demand he stop being everything I ever wanted from a guy. I want to warn him that if he continues to be this guy, I'll fall head over heels, so for his sake, he'd better show his asshole side fast or he'll be stuck with me along with Adeline.

I move one of his hands from my shoulder and step away from him. "Thank you, but I'm good. They'll just tense up again, so your wasting your time." I walk to the cupboard and grab a glass and fill it with water from the tap.

"I'm sorry for not helping with dinner," he says, and my thoughts of warning him off melt away.

"You were where you needed to be." I turn and give him a weak smile.

He leans against the island, staring at me. The look on his face is one I can't place into words. It's intense, searching mine for an answer to a question he has yet to ask. I can't take my eyes off him. He pushes off the island and moves across my kitchen and stands in front of me. He doesn't say a word but moves his hands to the sides of my neck, forcing me not to look away.

"I loved my brother, even when we didn't see eye to eye, but I never thought I could feel love like this before I came here."

"That's Adeline." I smile.

He rubs the back of my neck, slowly pulling me to him. I step forward, hating the distance between us. I want to burst into tears and ask him to want me, to stay with me. I rest my hands on his broad chest as the music of Stanaj floods my kitchen, giving voice to what I feel for Trevor Duncan—"Ain't Love Strange."

Out of nowhere, a tear falls onto my cheek.

5

TREVOR

The single tear that falls from Peggy's eye cuts me to the bone, ripping away my flesh and leaving me completely exposed. Her beautiful face, free of its frame of curls, looks so young and innocent… and mine.

"Talk to me."

I see her hesitation. It's so clear I can almost see her forming the details of her lie—so I wait. Resting my hands on her neck, rubbing her cheeks, soothing her, keeping her looking at me. I want her to open up to me, to jump and let me catch her.

She starts with, "I'm proud of Adeline. She has really come a long way." She licks her lips and avert her eyes from mine.

I tilt her head up slightly, forcing her to look at me again. "And…?"

"And… and… I… am going to miss her when the day comes that you leave."

I know she's holding back. I want to tell her I'm never leaving, that she will have me forever, that she is mine and I'm hers. However, the fear I see in her eyes—the fear she always has in her eyes, has me rethinking my approach. I want to hit the gas and speed through all the details that lead up to me telling her "I love you," but before I can do that, I have to find out what is holding her back. I know she feels something for me and I know it's not just lust.

"Trevor…"

"Peggy, I never thought I could feel love like this before meeting you."

She's standing in front of me, her expression stunned, and that's the exact reaction I was hoping for. I need to shock Peggy, get her talking, forcing her to face what we have between us if I ever want to get through to her. Her lips part and my stomach flips with nervous waves, anxious for her reply.

"Pizza!" Adeline screeches, followed by a series of noises I think are happy ones while she jumps up and down in front the island.

My gaze returns to Peggy's eyes, because she tells me so much of what she's feeling through those spheres of beauty and they look bewildered, but she also looks so lovely, which makes me smile. I'll leave her with those words to marinate on.

∽

MY LIFE in the last week has been more enjoyable and fulfilling than in the past fourteen years—no fuck that, my past life, period. Something as simple as homemade pizza filled my heart with joy. I can see why pizza-and-movie Saturday is Adeline's favorite thing in the whole, wide, entire world—her exact words.

I think I've learned more now than in the last fourteen years. I learned that little girls have many small, fragile keepsakes and placing a lamp is not as easy as you think. I've learned that I'm not artistic and my big fingers will never hold a paintbrush successfully—also her words. To run it down: you can never use too much red or yellow when painting, iced tea is better with a cherry, pizza needs extra everything to make it the best, and I love how I feel behind these walls.

The last fourteen years of my life I've been trying to find my purpose, to find what has been a miss in my life since my mother passed away. I've been searching for the one thing to fill that emptiness inside me, and I believe my search is finally over.

Peggy has yet to bring up that I professed my love for her, but she held my gaze all through dinner. On occasion, I catch her blushing, and I want to touch her warm cheeks and kiss her dizzy. The need to be with her grows more unbearable with every second, but I'm willing to play it cool. I don't want to push Peggy and risk chasing her away. She wouldn't get very far anyway. The feelings rushing through my body are so strong, it's a wonder I haven't exploded into a billion pieces.

"I never thought kiddy movies could be this entertaining," I say while collecting our dishes from our pizza dinner.

"Shh, Princess Tiana is getting ready to wish on the star." Adeline reprimands me then goes back to reciting her favorite Disney movie word for word.

I zip my lip and lock it tight with my imaginary key as Adeline smiles at my foolishness. I lift the tray of dishes and turn to walk into the kitchen.

"I'll help you and get the pie and ice cream," Peggy whispers, so as not to disturb Adeline's theatrical debut.

I step aside and allow her to walk ahead, admiring the sway of her hips and the bounce of her ass, so nice and round in another pair of small shorts. I look down at her bare feet and smile when I see her tiptoe to reach for the ice cream in the freezer. She sets it on the now-empty tray, along with three spoons, whipped topping, and a cooled pie. I'm leaning against her cabinet, watching her move around her kitchen, smiling every time she balances on pink-polished tippy-toes.

I'm not claiming to know the first thing about the world of fashion, but I do know beauty and I see how Peggy could sustain a successful career in modeling. The woman has an awareness of her body like none I've ever seen. Even when she's not conscious of it, she commands her body effortlessly, like a conductor commanding an orchestra.

I'm harder than I've ever been in my life, but the ache in my pants pales in comparison to the ache of longing I feel in my chest. I never gave a family much thought before, because of how fucked up mine was, but Peggy reminds me of the good times, before my mother was sick and my father an asshole. She makes me want things I never thought were important or realistic for my life.

She places napkins on the tray before resting her palms on the counter of the island with her head bowed. Her eyes are closed, and she takes a few deep breaths. I stand straight, ready to rush to her because she looks too defeated and worn out to stand much longer. But before I can spring into action, Peggy is in my arms. She wraps me in an embrace so tight, it feels as though she's steadying herself.

"I don't understand what's happening to me, what's happening between us. One minute I'm placing a pie on the tray. The next, I just need to be in your arms. I feel like my body's frequency is tuned directly to yours and you sent out a distress signal impossible to ignore." She whispers into my chest, and her body relaxes when I hold her close. "I'm not good with this kind of stuff." She buries her face in my chest, hiding from me as if she's embarrassed. "I've never been in love before. I've only ever had one boyfriend, and he turned out to be a monster."

I close my eyes and fight through the many meanings behind that statement. What kind of person could be anything but putty in her hands? I want her to explain, but I'm afraid of what she'll say and what I would do next. *I have the time and resources to dedicate to ending this person's life, and I wouldn't hesitate.*

Her soft sigh pulls me from my thoughts. "He's the reason I quit modeling."

I kiss the top of her head and pull her closer, wanting to reassure she's safe.

"I was very young, and I thought I knew it all. He was a fashion photographer, rich, and well connected in the industry. When I told him I wasn't ready for sex, he told me it was time to grow up."

My body tenses and my hold on her has tightened. When she

raises her beautiful brown eyes, scrutinizing me, I'm not sure what she sees when she looks at me, but I know what I'm feeling and rage is too tame of a word.

She must see the emotion because she places a hand on my cheek. "My best friend, Jess, barged in in time, and I only suffered a ridiculously hard slap to the face and an even harder blow to my trust in people, my trust in men. Until you. Until you, I never held on to a man for dear life. Until you, I never wanted a man so intimately. Until you, I wasn't ready for sex. Until you, I never knew what love felt like, what being in love feels like. Until you, I never would have thought I would ever say I love you, that I'm in love with anyone."

"I'm in love with you. The moment I laid eyes on you, I fell head over heels," I say. "Matter of fact, the moment I heard your voice over the phone, something inside me stirred to life. I had no doubt that Adeline was safe with you. I was anxious to be here, but it wasn't until I stood in your doorway, that I understood where the anxiety was coming from, what was causing it. Knowing that my brother—the last person in the world that loved me—was taken from me, the loneliness that hit me was an actual burning pain consuming my insides. Watching you and Adeline, the pain eased but the heat intensified, and my heart began beating life back into my body because I finally found what I was searching for. I found my lifeline, my forever. My heart knew it when I heard your first hello."

She raises up on tiptoe and nuzzles the line of my jaw with the tip of her nose. My lids flutter, absorbing the warmth and energy coursing through me from her. A groan disturbs the quiet, and I realize it came from me.

"Sorry," she says and lowers to the flats of her feet.

I kiss her forehead and squeeze her a little harder. "Come on, Adeline is enjoying her favorite movie alone."

"I know, I'm sorry. You make it hard to keep my hands to myself."

She smiles up at me, and this whole scene feels like the rest of my life. Peggy in my arms feels like the rest of my life, and I can't hold back any longer. I lean down to take her lips with mine, but I keep our connection brief. Her lips are full and soft, and I struggle to keep my tongue from exploring further. I pull away when she grinds against me. I hiss through my teeth and squeeze her hips, quickly losing my internal struggle.

"Woman, the things you can get me to do."

"I'm sorry."

I plant a quick kiss on her lips. "Never apologize for wanting me, because I will never be sorry for wanting you." I take one last quick kiss before gently smacking her right ass cheek. "Let's eat dessert before I eat you."

She gasps, and a blush lights up her face.

I smile and turn her away from me, walking us back to the island where I grab the tray. "Ladies first."

~

I WATCHED the ending of the movie alone. After finishing the pie and ice cream, Adeline crawled onto the sofa and snuggled with one of Peggy's decorative pillows and a blanket. She dozed off quickly. I'm sitting on the floor, propped against the front of Peggy's sofa with my legs outstretched and Peggy sitting between them, her back against my chest.

After learning that she was left physically, emotionally, and mentally bruised, her trust shaken, I couldn't let her go. I had to have her close enough that I could feel her warmth, have the vibrations from her laughter touch my heart.

She dozed off minutes after Adeline did, her head on my chest while I rubbed her arm. I turn my head from the credits rolling up the TV screen and kiss Adeline's forehead. Peggy's house is still and quiet. The lights are off, only the wall sconces in the stairwell and the ones flanking the fireplace illuminate her home. I bask in the moment, in the feelings overwhelming me. Love, peace, comfort, passion course through me, along with pure elation over this blessing in the wake of a sad situation. I have Adeline. I have Peggy. Now I need to work toward making all of this permanent.

It takes some maneuvering, but I'm able to stand while still holding Peggy. I make my way to her bedroom without waking her. She stirred a little at the sound of a squeaky floorboard, but when I lay her in her bed, she fists my shirt and whispers my name. I shush her and plant a kiss on her forehead. I have to tuck Adeline into bed, shut down the house, and shower.

I make my way down to get Adeline. I pick her up, and she's dead weight in my arms. I make my way up to her room. I turn on her Minnie Mouse lamp and kiss her forehead one last time before pulling the door, leaving it slightly ajar. I peek in on Peggy and see that her bed is empty, but I hear the shower and welcome the images of her naked and wet, rubbing soap over her caramel skin. I adjust the bulge in my pants and head downstairs to clean up, too.

I make quick work in the shower, avoiding the urge to rub one out. I vow to only release cum inside Peggy from here on out. I slip on a pair of boxer briefs, black basketball shorts, and a muscle shirt. I usually sleep naked, but that has changed since I'm not alone anymore. I pull my dreads up in a hair tie before checking every door and window downstairs. As I walk through the front rooms, I notice Peggy doesn't have an alarm.

Why the hell doesn't she have security?

I shake off the irritation creeping up my spine. How is it possible a single female with trust issues can live alone in a large house with no alarm service? The thought of someone invading her space and hurting her has me fuming. *Well, that changes first thing Monday morning.*

The thought settles my anger some, and when I'm satisfied that her home is locked up tight, I make my way to the guest room, despite my desire to head back up to Peggy's bedroom and give her a good night kiss. Finding out that my woman is still holding onto her cherry made every inch of my body hard. The thought of her pussy belonging only to me drives me wild with anticipation.

It's going to be pure hell trying not to fuck Peggy before I make her my wife.

Noises coming from the kitchen has me walking past the staircase instead of down the hallway to my room. I curse under my breath. If Peggy had an alarm I would have known if someone entered her home through any of the French doors she has in every room off the veranda.

Slowing my approach to the kitchen's entrance, readying myself to attack whoever decided to enter her home, I hear a whispered curse in the voice I first fell in love with. I move further in and stand in the doorway.

Peggy's rich cinnamon skin is draped in a cream-colored, thigh-length, strappy silk nightgown. The way the fabric covers her curvy frame, hugging all the right areas, is calling to me in the most intimate way. Her curly hair is once again framing her beautiful face, full and falling past her shoulders to the middle of her back. I push forward, anxious to be by her side.

She's leaning against the island with her curvy ass sticking out, and a mug of something hot next to her cell phone in her hand. It's not until I'm closer that I see she's texting.

My eyes move to the clock on the microwave. It's after ten in the evening, and I wonder who's so important that she had to reach out so late at night. I stand a safe distance away, keeping her unaware I'm in the room. I like watching her when her guard is down. She shows me details she would normally hide when aware of watchful eyes.

She frowns at the screen and pauses mid reply. Her thumbs hover over the phone before the right one taps rapidly in the same place. I assume she's deleting her words. I've never cared about a woman's dealings before, but my curiosity is about to get the best of me.

You've never been in love either, I remind myself.

With that, I realize in the right situation or better yet with the right woman—my woman—I'm one jealous bastard.

I lightly clear my throat, alerting her of my presence, so she's not startled. We've seen what can happen if she is, and I don't trust her with that hot beverage so close. She twists around and looks at me. "It's late, and you look beautiful and well rested, Ms. Jordan. Why the frown?" I stand next to her and see she's drinking hot tea.

She looks at her phone then back at me.

"I noticed I had several missed calls from my sister." She looks at her phone again. When she looks back at me, her teeth are worrying her bottom lip. "She texted me a few times, too."

"So what's the deal with your sister that has you so concerned?"

"She knows you're here."

"And?"

"And… well…"

"May I?" I hold out my hand. "Unless it's personal?"

"No, no, it's fine."

"Are you sure? I didn't mean to sound pushy."

"Trevor, you didn't. Please take it." She hands the phone to me.

I take her phone, prop my hip against her island, and push the button to bring it to life. Her screensaver is a picture of her and Adeline in formal attire. Peggy's standing so I see her profile, and her natural curls are styled straight and cascading down her back, barely touching the top of her ass. Adeline is in her arms, smiling, but the light that I normally see in her eyes is absent in this photo. I assume this picture was taken shortly after she came to live with Peggy.

"This is a beautiful picture of the two of you."

She looks over and smiles. "That was taken months ago at my sister's wedding. Adeline had only been with me a few weeks. She's changed so much in two and a half months. It's really amazing how far she's come."

"I can tell."

"It's the eyes, right?"

"Yes, it's the eyes. She has a light in them now that's missing here. You've done good, Ms. Jordan, and you are fucking stunning in this picture. Curly, straight, it doesn't matter, you are one beautiful woman." I lean close, bringing us eye to eye and whisper, "And you're mine."

I kissed her earlier this evening in almost this same spot. Our connection was brief, my sampling of her soft lips slight, but it was meant for comfort, after she confided in me a dark moment in her life. The exact moment that shaped the rest of her life thus far, forcing her to shield herself from ever being loved properly.

I take a minute and stare at her face. Her eyes burn with flames of desire and her cheeks are adorned with a sweet blush. Her lips are full, soft, and ready for another kiss, but the next time I taste Peggy's lips, I won't stop there, I'll taste the rest of her body. But right now she has a problem and we'll figure it out, together. I turn to the phone, swipe my finger across the screen, and read their text conversation.

Clarisse Price: Ignoring me! The only reason I'm not banging on your front door is because we talked earlier and I know Addie's uncle is in town. But I'm leaving you with this question… why the fuck didn't you tell me he was hot?! I got that tidbit of info from a five-year-old. I should really talk to Nana Joyce about those soaps she watches during the day. Riley around here calling men stud muffins! SMDH

"SMDH?" I ask.

"An acronym for shaking my damn head." I hear the amusement in her voice. "They don't SMDH in third world countries?"

"I'm sure they do, but I didn't have a cell phone." I continue reading.

Peggy: NO! I was enjoying Saturday night fun time… pizza and a movie! I didn't think you needed to know MRS. PRICE! How's Dylan doing? [smiley face]

Clarisse Price: WOW a jab… feeling protective Ms. Jordan? If you'd told me earlier, I would've said PLAY NICE. We all know how you can be.

Peggy: Don't start with me young lady.

Clarisse Price: You know that tone stopped working with me ages ago sister dear. What's the deal Pegs? The grapevine is talking and by that I mean your niece, and from what I hear, you are very cozy with Mr. Uncle. I was asked if he's your boyfriend… correction… "Our uncle too?"

Peggy: [smiley face]

Clarisse Price: WTF a smiley face? You had better start explaining Peggy!

"WTF?" I ask.

"What the fuck," she answers, and I smirk.

Clarisse Price: I want to meet him…tomorrow?

The last message came in over thirty minutes ago. I'm wondering what Peggy's been thinking about for so long. I wonder if she's not ready for a relationship, which would cause some real problems, because in my mind, we're already picking out rings and china patterns or whatever else women flip over. But I don't want to come right out and start accusing her of anything. I have to feel her out.

I look her way and she's placing her mug in the sink. "You think I'm hot?"

"Do you ever look in the mirror?"

"No, I don't always have one, why?"

She's back at my side now and slaps my shoulder, but her hand lingers longer than necessary. "If you haven't been paying attention, Mr. Duncan, yes, I think you're hot. Also, I trust my niece's opinion, and if she claims you're a stud muffin, then it must be true." She raises on tiptoe and kisses my cheek. I feel heat from my gut raise to my face and my dick stiffens. Peggy is the only woman who makes an innocent kiss on the cheek seductive.

"This last message was over thirty minutes ago. Do you have reservations about this?" I wave a finger between us.

Her eyebrows lift in shock, and she shakes her head. "No! Have you really not been paying attention? I'm just nervous."

"Of me meeting your family?"

"No, of answering questions, of explaining myself. I don't have the reputation of being lovable, soft, or understanding."

"But you are lovable and soft," I say. The woman she described was not the woman I'd come to know.

"There are a select few people who really know me, but my family aren't in that select few. Clarisse and I didn't grow up together." She walks to the fridge. "You want something?"

"No, I'm good."

She grabs a water bottle. "I started modeling when she was a baby. Before she started pre-school, I was traveling, and by the time she was old enough for us to bond, I was living abroad. When I returned to the States, I was living on campus, then after graduation, got my own place. Shortly after that, I became Clarisse's legal guardian and had to raise her. I had to be responsible and cutthroat to protect her and myself. I couldn't do that if I lost my head over a man or allowed her to do so." She shifted uncomfortably, and I could see her struggling to continue. "After what happened with… what happened to me, I erected a wall of protection. I equipped myself with the tools I needed to keep myself safe and vowed never to make the same mistake again."

She's now standing on the opposite side of the kitchen rolling the unopened water bottle between her hands. She wasn't kidding about those protective walls. She just put distance between us, and I'm positive she's unaware that's what she did. *Oh, my angel.*

"The problem is, my walls kept everyone out."

She looks bewildered by what to do next and a little sad, which brings a pain to my chest. I want Peggy to break out of this hard shell and spread her wings, because she has so much more to give. I open her phone again and smile at the photo before I swipe the screen and type: Lunch?

Peggy pushes off the cabinet and leans over the island in front of me, and I try not to stare at the tops of her breast spilling out the night gown while she reads the message I just sent. She looks at me with anxiety in her eyes.

"Peggy, baby, I'll be with you. You can't hide forever. I'll be with you," I say.

She looks at her phone the same time it pings.

Clarisse Price: Damn Peggy! You took your time! Lucky for you Dylan is a master at distracting me. LOL… Lunch sounds good. I'll text Rhonda and Connor too. Should we bring something?

"Huh?" I look her way for an answer.

She covers her face and groans. "What have I gotten myself into?"

"It'll be okay, baby." I reply to her sister that lunch is covered. I slide her back the phone, and she leaves it where it on the countertop.

"I'm sure it will be fine, but I'm still nervous." She picks up the water bottle—still unopened—and begins rolling it between her hands again. I want to pick her up and ask her to marry me and be my forever. Instead, I give her what she needs right now…release.

I walk over to her and take the water bottle from her hands and place it on the counter. I slide my hands around her waist and lift her up. "Wrap your legs around my waist."

She does, and I carry her to the family room where I sit on the sofa. I rub her back with one hand while keeping the other on her neck, making sure she stays with me. I don't want to miss a thing. I want to kiss her, but that would prevent me from seeing into her soul, and I want her heart and soul, forever.

She leans forward and nuzzles my nose with hers, giving me Eskimo kisses. She scoots closer and her warm uncovered center rests against my hard cock, and I groan, part relief, part agony. I know she feels how hard I am because she grinds her hot center on me. I continue to rub her back, giving her encouragement. The scent of her arousal engulfs me, and I'm dizzy with the need to claim her, but the timing isn't perfect, and I want to establish an understanding between us before we move forward. I need her to know that I'm it for her, just as she is for me.

I grip her hips to halt her movements and thrust upward, rubbing my covered hard piece against her pussy under her silk night gown. The hand on her neck pulls her to my chest and I hold her there. She moans, and I thrust once more, wanting to pull another from her lips.

"You are my weakness, and all I want right now is to enjoy this time with you. The scent of your arousal drives me crazy, and I would move through hell to make you orgasm and intensify the scent of you." I cup her cheeks, lift her face from my chest, and stare into her eyes. I want to see her eyes when she lets go, but Peggy had another idea.

"You're a drug," she says, "and all I want to do is overdose."

"I want to kiss you so badly, but one little taste will never satisfy me. A little attention from you will never be enough. I want all of your attention. I want to be important to you, and I want to be your world, because you are mine."

"You're mine, Trevor and I'm yours."

My control snaps and I stand straight up from the sofa with her still clinging to my body. I place her on her back on the sofa. The silk fabric pools around her hips and her pussy plays peek-a-boo below the hemline. I adjust myself as her scent still swarms my head and I feel the evidence of her wetness on my shorts and my mouth waters. She's looking up at me, a halo of chestnut curls a backdrop, framing her face. She's all soft eyes, flushed cheeks and full parted lips. Her beauty is almost intimidating. I drop to my knees, ready to worship her.

"This is purely for your pleasure, Peggy." I wrap my hands around her ankles and begin a slow move up her calves to her knees. I slip my fingers between her thighs and slowly begin to separate them. As I suspect, her cunt is bare and glistens from her arousal.

"Damn Peggy, you have a beautiful pussy."

"Trevor…"

Her breathy whispers are cut short when I give her pussy a kiss. Strawberries, that's how I'd describe Peggy's flavor. She squirms and moans, whispering my name whenever I tongue kiss her tight hole or suck her clit. She says I'm a drug she wants to overdose on, and I feel the same about the taste of her. I could easily get addicted to her flavor.

I'm like a starved animal feasting on her until her back bows, gripping my locs, holding me to her sweetness—as if I would really miss the chance to drink her down to the last drop.

"You're killing me, Ms. Jordan," I whisper against her quivering cunt.

I lower my head to get closer to her sweetness and place one last kiss there before I pull away and stand. If I don't stop now, I'll never stop. My cock is hard enough to bore a hole through a cement wall.

I pull her up from the sofa, because she looks too good to ignore. "This is all I can take right now, baby. With these strong emotions rushing through me, if we move any further, I'll take you right now."

"But you make my body ache with needs I've ignored my entire adult life. When I'm near you, in your arms, I want to feel you everywhere, deep inside me, consuming me, pleasing me." Her voice quivers with need." I want to please you, too. I want you crazy hot for me like I am for you."

Her arms wrap around my neck, and I close my eyes and absorb the sensation of her gentle contact and her soft skin surrounding me. I'm much taller, so I bend forward and she pulls me closer, wrapping me further into her embrace. She briefly tastes my lips, indulging in a sample of her essence from them. I fist my hands at my sides in an attempt to avoid grabbing her.

"Mercy," I whisper across her lips. "Have mercy on me. I'm only so strong, woman."

She giggles and nuzzles my neck, giving me one last squeeze before she releases me, and I immediately miss her warmth. I escort her to the bedroom.

Her bed is on the far side of the room and faces the doorway. In the middle of an all-white palette, with touches of soft grays and dark beiges, I pick her up and sit Peggy in her bed.

"Stay with me. I've never had this before. I can't help but be selfish," she says.

"This is pretty new for me, too," I say. The look in her sleepy eyes is the most seductive ever aimed my way. Peggy makes me feel ten feet tall.

She flips the bed covers down, welcoming me to join her, and I don't hesitate. As soon as I rest my back on the pillows, Peggy nestles into me. I wrap my arm around her and pull her closer, kissing the top of her head and turn off the lamp, which leaves the room is complete darkness. I can't remember the last time I slept in a bed so comfortable.

"I love this," Peggy whispers into my neck and wiggles closer to me. She wraps her arms around my waist and slides a hand under my shirt to rub my back.

I shiver and push my groin against her. She moans, and I groan at my carelessness.

Sex has never been an intimate act for me. It was fun and exciting until my mid-twenties, then it just became something to do when I was lonely. The last seven years, I would hit the autopilot switch in my brain, so my body would remain present but my mind would go somewhere else altogether. I'd barely remember the chick suckered into whatever I was peddling. It's been so long since I've had a full erection, my dick feels foreign to me.

I would love to strip Peggy bare and lick every inch of her sweet skin and eat her delicious pussy to orgasm again, making her soft, warm, wet, and ready for my cock to claim her cherry. I would do anything to lose myself in the embrace of her arms and legs while I ride her slow and deep until she screams my name.

But I want our coupling to mean something, so I need to pull back, but she's making that impossible, wrapped around me and feeling so warm and soft. The scent of whatever soap or lotion she uses—and I still taste her on my tongue—has my head dizzy and my body hard. I'm searching my mind for anything I can use to cool this down, but find nothing. I should get the hell out of her bed and go downstairs where I belong, but like a true dumbass, I climbed into bed with the biggest temptation in my life.

"Peggy?" I whisper hoarsely. Her lips have found a spot on my neck I never knew had a direct connection to my cock. "Fuck, is this really what you want now?"

I'm praying that somewhere inside her, she holds the notion of "no sex before marriage" in high regard, because I need something to slow this down. However, the way she's grinding her pussy on me, I don't think she does.

"You've waited all this time. Don't you want it to be special?" I ask, my voice sounding strained even to my own ears.

She lifts her head and makes direct eye contact with me. She moves quickly, straddling me with her hands firm on my chest, as if she's holding me down. My eyes have adjusted to the darkness, so I see the heat in them threating to burn me alive.

"You're special, and that's all the special I need." Before I have time to react, she's pushing my shirt up my chest, and I help by dragging it over my head. She bites her bottom lip. "Oh, you are so beautiful and so fucking sexy." Her greedy hands roam all over my abs, chest, and arms. "Your skin is so soft, yet you're so hard." She's folds forward and kisses my neck in the same spot as before, and my dick jerks in my shorts.

Her name comes out a strained groan as I try to catch my breath. "I'm trying my hardest to do right by you."

"If the right thing is what you want," she whispers, then nips my ear lobe, "you should've never kissed my pussy." She sits up, leaving me panting.

She removes her nightgown, and I moan at the sight of her naked body. "Oh shit, Peggy, you little minx."

Her body is more beautiful than I ever imagined, curving in at the waist and flaring out at her wide hips. Her breasts are lush, capped with caramel nipples so full and taut, begging for my mouth.

I squeeze my eyes shut, attempting to control myself, but my hands aren't on the same page. I palm her full breasts. My body moving without permission, I grab her waist and lift her to my lips, placing a kiss on her stomach. I sit up all the way, bringing us eye to eye now, and I see her determination shooting like daggers at me. A full realization of the situation slams into me. She wants this, and I surrender to her.

"I love you so fucking much," I proclaim and take her mouth in the kiss I've been holding back all day. Scratch that, the kiss I've been holding back all week. Peggy raises from my lap to her knees and deepens our connection. I take long licks at her mouth, seizing the opportunity her raised ass gives me to struggle with my shorts and boxers, freeing my cock.

She tastes so sweet, and her moans are driving me insane with need. I'm lost in this kiss, and my exposed cock stands rock-hard and probing her hot, wet center. I grab two handfuls of the soft flesh of her ass and grind her against my throbbing cock. I thrust upward, rubbing her hard clit, while she uses me to rub out an orgasm.

I try to steady her as she takes what she needs, but she gets away from me and shifts her hips, slamming down the same time I thrust up, and my cock pushes through her tight flesh, claiming her virgin cherry. She freezes and lets out a tremulous gasp, her face contorting into a mask of pleasure-pain.

Her fingers dig into my shoulders and she throws her head back, riding me, her pussy squeezing my cock the hardest I've ever felt as an orgasm rushes through her body. I pull her close and hold her while she rides the wave of her pleasure, adjusting to the size of my cock deeply embedded into her tight, hot cunt.

If Peggy ever intended to take things slow with us, she just destroyed that notion. My fingers smooth down the slope of her back and grab onto her fleshy ass again. I can only hope and pray she's ready for what she has unleashed, because now nothing in the world will stop me from claiming Peggy completely.

6

PEGGY

I can't speak, think, even breathe.
 Laying on top of Trevor's hard chest, I can only feel, and what I'm feeling is powerful and all-consuming. The mix of pain and pleasure is intoxicating. Tears stream from my eyes, the only way to release some of this energy. An orgasm is still rolling through my body, and the feeling is addictive. I shudder through it. Trevor is so big, he's stretching me, filling my insides, and I want more.

"Please." I finally release my breath with one word, and now I have room to absorb everything Trevor is doing to me.

His lips are on my neck. He kisses down to my breasts, and a zing of pleasure hits me right in my core as he latches onto a nipple. I groan and work my hips up then down, sliding his thick cock deeper inside me, and I realize I'm on top of him and can do what I want. I slow down, trying to gain my bearings, working my body on his.

"Take what you want, baby, I'm yours."

His voice hits deep inside me, and I feel greedy because I want all of it and I'm not even sure what *it* is. With my hands on his chest, I caress him, worshiping all the exposed skin my fingers touch. I brush my fingertips over his nipples and his muscles tighten under my palms. His cock jerks inside me, his upward thrust hitting that sweet spot inside, and I explode again.

"That's it, baby. Oh, damn, you're so tight, so hot. You're squeezing the fuck out of my dick."

I cry out and he takes my mouth, silencing me, but the feel of his tongue massaging mine adds to my pleasure and I clench him harder, riding through my orgasm. Trevor trails open-mouth kisses down my neck as I come down from my second high, and my limbs feel like jelly. I rest my temple against his as he loves on my neck. His lavender scent invades my senses and relaxes me further. I'm riding him slowly, feeling his size in every slide of his cock into my body.

"I love you," I whisper into the darkness, willing the impact of my words to engulf us, creating a bubble that we can remain in forever.

"What those words do to me." I feel is smile against my collarbone. He grips my hips, halting my movement, guiding me to hover over him, as he thrusts upward. "I want one more orgasm, baby. Can you give your man what he wants?"

"Oh, God," I moan. His words driving me onward, I feel my core tighten.

"I love you, my angel. I want forever with you—shit, you're close, I can feel it."

"Oh, Trevor," I say, delirious with pleasure. My body is slick with sweat, my hair clinging to my back and neck. "I want to come. Baby, make me come, please make me come."

He growls and squeezes my ass, plunging in and out of me faster and so deep. My whimpers are in rhythm with the slapping sounds of our bodies. He slows to a steady pace.

As I catch my breath he says, "I'm not pulling out. I'll always come inside you. Are you on the pill, taking the shot, anything that will prevent pregnancy?"

"No, I've never needed to. You're the first man I ever wanted this with."

"And I'm the only man you ever will have this with." His

possessive words are laced with anger at the idea of another man touching me. "I want a life with you, and a family."

I gaze in his eyes and see the sincerity in his promise of a life I've always wanted but gave up hope in ever having because of one man's dark soul and violent blows.

He moves his hands over my ass, a soothing caress, before he picks up speed again, plunging deeper inside me. My walls are tight, and the push and pull of his thick cock is driving me insane. I shift forward and take his mouth, devouring him. At this angle, his pelvic bone applies pressure against my clit, and I meet his thrusts with a quick roll of my hips. The pleasure is building. I release his lips, and he's staring at me with so much determination.

"Oh, Trevor, I'm coming." I'm so hot from his words and the thought of taking his seed, my belly round with his baby, pushes me over the edge.

I whimper as I fall apart again. Through the rush of blood clogging my ears, I hear Trevor grunting and I feel the warmth of his release. It's so much, his cum drips out of me. Trevor moves with lightning speed and my back presses into the mattress. He's hovering over me, still filling me, grunting and moaning, and I can't stop staring at his beautiful face. His forehead creasing, those light eyes razor sharp and focused on my face. He tilts my bottom up, pulling out so the tip of his cock is still inside me, almost as if he's attempting to plug my entrance.

He's frowning in concentration. "I don't want any to leak out."

"We can always try again," I say, smiling at him. I love the idea of having him whenever I want him, and I'm planning to want him always.

∽

WHEN I'M NOT PANTING and squirming with pleasure, we talk and laugh and touch one another. Keeping my fingers off his smooth skin is nearly impossible, and he seems to have the same issue, which I don't mind one bit. Trevor keeps me on my back, legs open wide, massaging my clit with gentle strokes of his fingertips.

He kisses and nibbles all over my body, though my breasts receive most of his attention. He brings me to orgasm another couple times until I can't keep my eyes open. The last thing I remember before I surrender to sleep is Trevor placing soft kisses on my lips. There's no better way to be welcomed into dreamland.

The next morning, I open my eyes slowly, feeling the weight of my lids. I feel well rested, but don't feel like moving. I'm alone in my bed, with sheets that smell of lavender and sex, and I want to remain wrapped in them all morning, but my family is coming for lunch today. It's eight o'clock when I slip from my bed covers. The ache in my muscles reminds me I'm no longer a virgin, and I blush beet red.

I remove my bedding, toss it in the hamper, and pull fresh sheets from the dresser drawer. Once my bed's made, I head to the bathroom and hop in the shower. Trevor promised last night not to leave my side, so I don't know why I'm so nervous—correction, scared to death. There is a lot about me that my family doesn't know. I never dreamed of telling my sister what happened with the-man-whose-name-I-dare-not-speak. I've never allowed myself to be placed in the hot seat, and with this impending family lunch, my ass feels rather warm.

Taking a deep breath, I open my closet and grab a gray-and-white floral-print maxi dress. Then I hit my lashes with a little mascara and apply pink gloss to my lips. My hair is styled in an over-the-shoulder braid before making my way downstairs.

"Good morning, Peggy," Adeline yells over the *Jungle Book* soundtrack playing through the downstairs sound system. She's at the island, hard at work on another picture.

She's changed so much since she first arrived at my house. She was withdrawn, so I introduced drawing as a way to explore her feelings and open up to me. I've learned about Adeline through her art, and one thing that stands out is that she and her mother were not close—correction, they were totally estranged.

Adeline calls her Traci more than she calls her mom. I think that lack of affection is why Adeline took to me so quickly. How she explains her pictures, I have no doubt that she was a daddy's girl. I'm still not sure how her mother could have starved this beautiful little girl of simple things like hugs and kisses. I kiss the top of her head before opening the refrigerator so I can start on her breakfast.

"I ate pancakes! Uncle Trevor made me two of them with lots and lots of honey, cinnamon, and blueberries. They were yummy." She looks up from her drawing, a thoughtful expression on her face. "You know, I think the man knows how to cook."

I smile with her. "Yes, I do believe your uncle can cook."

I scan the kitchen and notice he's cleaned after himself. In my butler pantry, at the Keurig, I pop in a pod and select my cup size. Strong hands slide around my waist at the same time his warm lips graze the side of my exposed neck, and my body goes up in flames.

"Good morning, angel. You look beautiful," he whispers in my ear and hugs me close. His hard body against mine has me wanting more than a morning greeting. "I'm sorry you woke up alone. Adeline wanted pancakes and I decided to let you sleep, seeing as you had a very long, pleasurable, exhausting night." As he speaks, he trails kisses along my neck, and I'm relieved we're tucked away from young impressionable eyes.

I turn in his arms and wrap mine around his neck, smiling at him. "Why thank you for the workout, the extra rest, and the compliment."

"Workout?"

"Yes, my muscles are quite sore, Mr. Duncan, but my heart is so full of love."

He places a kiss to the tip of my nose. "Are you hungry?"

Without releasing me, he lifts the lid on my warming plate and I spot pancakes with three sausage links on the side. My stomach rumbles.

He grabs the plate and escorts me to the kitchen table. "Sit, eat, and I'll get your coffee."

He brings my cup, and I take a sip and moan in appreciation for the strong rich flavors.

"Enjoy your meal, Ms. Jordan. I'll be in the shower," he says.

I turn to check him out. He's still wearing the muscle shirt and basketball shorts from last night, and in the light of day, he blows my mind. I lick my lips, hungry for something other than breakfast.

"Food, Peggy. Remember your sore muscles. That look will get you in trouble." But he doesn't back away from me. Instead he leans down and gives me a deep, earth-shattering, too-early-for-this kind of kiss. I'm lost in it and forget Adeline's at the island. I reluctantly pull away and chance a glance her way. She's still hard to work on a new picture but I blush anyway. Trevor smiles. "Now eat, angel."

And with that, he walks to his room. I almost follow him because I can't eat after that kiss, until I notice Adeline staring at me. My blush deepens, embarrassed at what she may have witnessed of our display of affection.

"He loves you. I heard him say that on the phone while I was eating my pancakes."

Her declaration has me walking over to her. Who was he talking to? I don't remember him mentioning anyone important in his life. He said he has a best friend—Terry, I think he called him—but he also said he could only reach him through email and they check in every few weeks.

"Did you happen to hear who he was talking to?"

"No." She shakes her head and resumes working on her art. "He just kept saying, 'I'm done, I'm done,'" she says, mocking his tone.

I frown and bite my bottom lip. I look toward his room, and my feet move before my brain gives the order. I call over my shoulder, "Adeline, when you're finished with the picture, I placed a sundress on your bed."

"Can I wear my rain boots?"

"Not today squirt, bare feet will do."

She puffs out a breath of defeat and continues working. . I'm not even sure what I want to know or if I even have a right to know anything. I stand in the doorway of his room, my brain playing catch up.

I hear the shower and look around the room. Everything looks the same. I'm not sure what I was expecting. I guess because I feel different, I expect everything else to be different too.

I force myself onward, wanting to get answers to quiet the green-eyed monster growing inside me. The thought of Trevor being with anyone before me cramps my stomach. The thought that he could have still been with someone while he was inside me last night makes me nauseated.

The thought that he was talking to that person moments before he put his hands on me makes me enraged and I want to cry. I hate the feelings I can't seem to control, because it would be a lot easier for me to kick his ass out the front door—if I wasn't in love with him.

I look at my backyard through the window, and I long to be outside, feeling my long dress tangled at my ankles in the wind instead of dealing with these complicated feelings. My attention, moves to the desk near the window where Adeline's picture sits. It must be the picture Trevor commissioned her to create last night. I find myself looking through Adeline's eyes at her family—it's my family. Clarisse and her husband, Dylan; the twins, FJ and Riley; Clarisse's best friends, Rhonda and Connor; me, Adeline, and Trevor. She drew Trevor and me holding hands.

"I guess I'll be meeting them this afternoon." His voice fills the room.

"Yes, they'll all be here," I say, not turning from the picture.

"I like that she titled this one, 'My Family.' I'm beyond grateful to you and your family for loving her so much, and I look forward to the day I'm officially a member."

"Are you involved with someone?" I blurt, ignoring his last

words. I don't have the time or the patience to tiptoe around this issue. "Were you involved with someone?"

I rephrase the question because he may have broken that involvement off just this morning. I'm waiting with my back to him, my head downcast, my eyes closed, preparing for him to break my heart. I'm preparing for him to start with, "Let me explain," or to downplay his involvement with this woman... if there is a woman.

"Look at me," he demands.

I feel so defeated. "Just answer the question."

"Please," he whispers.

His tone has me doing as he asks. I have to still myself after I lay eyes on his half-naked body still wet from his shower. His long, light-brown dreads are loose and draped over his shoulders. A white towel barely covers his lower half, hanging off his hips.

The man's frame takes up the doorway of the bathroom, his body riddled with hard-defined muscle. He looks like a god—or with his intense scowl, a warrior. He eats up the distance between us with three steps, and now he's invading my personal space without a care. I'm forced to look up at him and I feel small again, but he doesn't intimidate me, not in the slightest. He turns me on, and that pisses me off.

"You have five seconds, Mr. Duncan," I say through clenched teeth.

"And that's all the time I need to get you naked and under me."

"Stop that," I growl. "Don't do that. I'm being serious." I fold my fingers over the edge of the desk, holding on as tight as I can. The last time I gave him a count of five he tossed me over his shoulder like a rag doll.

He frowns and bends to catch my glare. "Hey..." He moves closer, sliding his hand around the side of my neck and lifting my face so he can look into my eyes. He's trying to figure out what's wrong. "Angel, where is this coming from? I just left you to enjoy breakfast. I don't understand."

"Please answer the question." Emotion fills my voice.

"I have never been in a relationship in my life. To answer the question, Peggy, I'm not now, nor was I ever, involved with anyone." He lightly passes his soft, full lips over mine.

I close my eyes and absorb the feel of him and his familiar lavender scent. I've never known a man to smell so good. It has to be a hair care product, because the scent isn't on his skin. I turn my face, lean into the curtain of his dreads, and take a deep breath.

"Tell me what happened? What brought these questions on?" His lips press lightly against my cheek.

I need a minute to sort through the intense emotions that wrecked by mind, body, and soul just moments ago. I shake my head, feeling a little silly, but I do owe him an explanation. I hope he won't see me as some crazy lady and rethink our involvement.

"Adeline mentioned you were on a call repeatedly saying you were done, and… well… I assumed you where ending some previous thing with some woman, and the thought made me sick inside. I was so angry from the idea that the first time you were inside me, you really didn't belong to me."

"Oh, angel, I'm all yours. You have all of me. What I told you last night was no line or ploy to have sex with you. You are my forever. I'm yours, and you're mine."

"I'm so sorry for accusing you of being sleazy."

He laughs, and the sound is the elixir I need to bring me out of the darkness. Clutching his dreads, I pull his head to mine and take his lips in a passionate kiss, one that asks for forgiveness and promises so much more. "Do you forgive me, Mr. Duncan?"

"Yes, Ms. Jordan, you have my forgiveness." He kisses my lips once more, but this one is sweet and soft. "Just to make matters clear, I was talking to Braden's executive assistant. She left a message yesterday regarding an urgent matter that needs to be rectified involving the casino."

"Oh my, I hope it isn't serious."

"Mainly some loose ends that need to be tied up. I understand the urgency. However, I stood by my word when told her was taking these first few weeks to be with Adeline before I deal with casino business. She was giving me some shit explanation. But I'm not budging and I told her so."

"Is everything going to be okay?" My concern heightens but its selfishly charged. I'm not ready for them to up and move to Vegas. Trevor made some promises last night, but he never promised to be my forever right here is Savannah.

"The Golden Temple will survive. It's just my brother had a few deals in play, and the timing is important in closing these deals. That puts us in a difficult position, but giving me what I demand is non-negotiable." He kisses my lips once more and pulls me into him. I wrap his waist in a tight hug and burrow my face into his abs, inhaling his clean scent.

"I really do apologize for jumping to conclusions," I whisper against his smooth skin.

"I love you, Ms. Jordan," he says, then gives my ass a gentle swat. "Now go eat."

"You better be happy I'm hungry." I raise to tiptoe. He meets my lips with his and I give him another kiss, this one brief.

"I love you, Mr. Duncan." I moisten his lips with my words before I release my hold and make my way to the door. Pausing, I look back in time to see this sexy bastard drop the towel and begins to dress in front of me. This is my first good look at his body, and the sight of him makes me want to drop to my knees, beg, cry, and plead to have him again—let my inhibitions fall away and hit the floor with his towel. He continues to dress, covering every beautiful inch of his body. I watch in awe, but he's completely covered in jeans and a white T-shirt too soon for my liking. His dreads still loose, he picks me up again and brings me to the kitchen, where Addie is finishing her picture.

She smiles when she sees that I'm in Trevor's arms. "When are my cousins coming over?"

That's the first time she's ever referred to the twins as her cousins, and I wonder what she's thinking, what's going on in that pretty little head of hers.

"They'll be here in a few hours," Trevor answers as he places me on my feet.

I'm dumbfounded, still stuck in an eye-gasmic haze from watching Trevor slip jeans over his sexy ass, that I don't say anything. I just fall into step with him as he prepares lunch for my family.

7
TREVOR

The woman standing next to me, helping with the final touches to the fried chicken, bake macaroni and cheese, and garden green salad for the family lunch is the most amazing woman I've ever met. After she finished breakfast, she helped Adeline dress and drove her John Deere Gator TE ATV to her garden. With Adeline's help, they picked the veggies for the salad and enough flowers for a dozen centerpieces.

Before her family arrives, Peggy shared information about them. Her sister, Clarisse is pregnant and owns her own business, a café quickly on the rise. Her husband, Dylan, is the CEO of his family's multi-billion-dollar development corporation. Rhonda, Clarisse's best friend and like another little sister to Peggy, is a trust-fund brat, but she used to work for Dylan a short while before she left and returned to Atlanta where her family lives. Connor, Clarisse other best friend, is a programmer for a gaming enterprise and recently moved back to Georgia after living in Dubai the last three years.

I test my memory with the details. "Dylan and Clarisse married a few months ago and she's a few months pregnant. Dylan's the twins' step-father. Their father died when they were two?" She nods while slicing through one of the tomatoes Adeline picked. "Then there's Rhonda and Connor."

"Those two have layers of complicated issues," Peggy says, explaining their on and off relationship.

"I thought you said they were working things out."

"No, I wish they were. Just know this, those two are madly in love and have been since adolescence. They were involved before Connor left for Dubai. He's been back only three months and I'm not sure Rhonda will ever get her shit together concerning him." She dumps the tomatoes in the salad bowl before pointing a finger my way with the sexiest narrow-eyed frown. "Clarisse knows very little regarding her best friends involvement, and it's supposed to remain that way until Rhonda decides it should change."

"What could be that complicated?" I ask.

"It's not my place to tell. Not even the man I love."

She tippy-toes and quickly kisses my lips. I grab her hips and turn her to face me so I can have a proper taste of her sweet mouth. Peggy's plump lips light my fire and I'm craving her soft flesh. Before I grab a fist full of gray and white fabric, the doorbell rings throughout the house and announces her family. I whisper promises for later across her lips but can't help but smile when she groans in frustration.

∽

WHY WAS Peggy so nervous about this lunch? So far we've had a great time. The best time I've spent in a long time in the company of adults.

My first impression of the group is that they love and care for one another. After lunch, they dismissed the children from the table to the playroom Peggy set up upstairs, before they share stories and engage in harmless banter back and forth, all in the name of family fun. Some of the stories floating around the table may be embarrassing for Peggy, but I can't help but puff my chest with pride that she belongs to me.

According to the girls, Peggy is a razor-tongued, ruthless interrogator who in the past ran off more than one of Rhonda's boyfriends.

"After seven minutes in her company, Peggy had my prom date canceling on me a week before prom," Rhonda says.

"So you went without a date?"

"No," she answers, a smirk on her face.

"I took pity on her and volunteered to fill in," Connor adds. Rhonda gives him a stink-eye to his wide smile.

"And that wasn't the last dude she sent running for the hills. A dozen of her love interests may have lasted three dates, tops." Rhonda points her fork in Peggy's direction.

Peggy doesn't deny their claims. She gives a stern look and throws out a blunt response. "Those guys were complete morons."

"Her boyfriends are yours?" I turn to Peggy and ask.

"Both, but let's be clear, they were never my boyfriends."

"Mine were not..." Rhonda begins, but glances at Peggy. "Okay, maybe they were morons."

The entire group laughs.

"What about me?" Dylan asks. "She godfathered me when Clarisse and I started dating."

"Correction," Peggy answers. "You never dated my sister. You married my sister."

"And I'll never apologize for that. She's the best deal I ever made. If given a do-over, I wouldn't change a thing." Dylan plants a kiss on Clarisse's lips.

She blushes and whispers something in his ear that makes his smile widen.

"What about William?" Clarisse asks, reaching her fork over to snag a piece of Dylan's chocolate cake from his plate. He switches his plate with her empty one. She smiles and gives him a kiss.

"What about William?" I ask, their cute, in-love display distracts me a mere second. Peggy said he was a friend, never said they dated or that before he was her neighbor or good friend, he held the title of boyfriend. Peggy forks her cake nervously, pushing crumbles in a small pile.

"Peggy and he have been going back and forth for some time now." Clarisse says shoving the last fork full of dessert in her mouth. "He was the only one who past the third date, right Peggy?"

I try for a cool, relaxed demeanor, but fail when I sit back in my chair and cross my chest with my arms.

"That's right!" Rhonda says sitting up in her seat. "You're right Clari, they have a standing Thursday dinner date. He's hot, Peggy."

I almost flip the table. That good ol' boy has been dating my girl off and on for some time and he was in her house, flaunting his claim on her in front of my face? What the fuck?

Damn this shit hurts. I see why Peggy reacted the way she did earlier when she thought I was with someone.

"Not last Thursday," I add, not caring how my words come across.

The room goes quiet. I eye her family's reactions with one raised brow. Clarisse halts the cake knife halfway through cutting her third slice to stare at me, then looks at Rhonda. Rhonda's wide-eye gaze moves from Clarisse, and they both stare at Peggy, whose eyes are downcast, playing with her cake. Dylan has a smile on his face and Connor looks confused.

"So Riley was telling the truth," Clarisse says. "She said Aunt Peggy has a boyfriend. I thought she might be talking about William."

I take Peggy's hand, knowing how hard this is for her to open up to her family.

"Trevor and I…"

"OMG!" Clarisse blurts out. She abandon's her cake, clapping her hands and bouncing in her seat.

"Clarisse! She hasn't said anything yet," Rhonda points out.

"My wife is just excited for her sister." Dylan leans over and kisses her temple. "But we should hear her out, baby." He stares at Peggy and me, as is everyone at the table.

Peggy smiles at me. "It happened so fast."

"Shit, three months is fast for you, Peggy, but a week?" Rhonda stretches her hand across the table. "I have to shake the hand of the one man in this world who accomplished the impossible."

"My man." Dylan reaches behind Clarisse and grab my shoulder, giving a firm squeeze. "Welcome."

Peggy blushes, but she also never addresses Clarisse's statement regarding her and William, and I feel sick. Knowing she wasn't physically intimate with him does nothing to ease the jealousy. She may not have shared her body, but I can imagine what else she has shared with him: hugs, handholding, dinner dates, conversation, looks of longing, even a smile after sharing a kiss. I've never cared before what a woman did or didn't do before or after I had my time with her, but with Peggy, I'm a possessive, selfish bastard.

I make no excuses or apologies for wanting all of her smiles, her conversations, her soft touches, her complete attention. I try my hardest to shelve these stabbing pains to my heart and force myself to remain calm. Now is not the time for me to ask how friendly this next door neighbor has been with my angel. We'll talk later, but for now I push on and clear my throat before I speak.

"Now that we have everybody's attention, I would like to thank every one of you for welcoming my niece into this family. I didn't have the pleasure of knowing her, and I'm playing catch up, but because of this magnificent woman next to me, Adeline will have what her father and I had with our mother. My mother passed when I was in high school. She was the only light in my life, and when she was gone, so was I. I ran to the other side of the world in search of something that could restore the light she gave me." I'm still holding Peggy's hand, and I lean forward in my chair to dig the red James Avery box from my front pocket.

Gasps spill from the lips of the people around the table.

"Oh hell, not this shit again!" Rhonda slouches in her chair, applying finger pressure to her temples. "What is it with men wanting to marry after the first hello is exchanged?"

"Rhonda, that's not true. I wanted to marry Clarisse before the first hello," Dylan says.

I open the box and pull out a silver necklace, thinking a proposal is coming soon enough. Dangling from my hand is a nesting bird charm with a blue enamel egg and a turquoise bead. I have the same necklace for Adeline, which she'll get tonight before I put her into bed.

"I searched for fourteen years, only to find my light was here all along. My mother used to say, 'Thank God for angels' and, Peggy, that was the first thought that came to me when Jackson told me you'd taken in Adeline. Do you know the spiritual meaning behind a bluebird?"

She shakes her head, her eyes glistening with tears.

I link the necklace behind her neck and close the clasp. "She's the symbol of happiness." I take the charm in my hand. "Her songs are filled with simple pleasures and possibilities. It's said that if you're going through a dark time, the bluebird reminds us to hold on, that the situation will get brighter. She symbolizes the heavenly realm, and when she appears, it's a sign of loved ones in heaven. Bluebirds are the physical incarnations of angels. Peggy, you are my bluebird. You are Adeline's bluebird. My mother believed in angels on earth. She believed you were possible." I release the charm and cup her face, thumbing the tears from her cheeks. "Peggy, you will always be my angel."

"Oh my God," Clarisse whispers.

I pull Peggy into my arms and hug her close. I really want to place her in my lap and taste her tear-covered lips but settle for pulling her chair closer to mine. My gaze captures a blend of smiles and tears around the table. Clarisse is tearing up so intensely that Dylan pulls her into his lap and kisses her forehead. Rhonda is settled into Connor's side, her head on his shoulder and his arm around her.

"Trevor, I must say, you sure know how to get everyone's attention," Connor says, nodding toward Rhonda. She appears to be sad. I don't get much of an opportunity to examine her body language further because Peggy takes my hand.

"Trevor, I love it. Thank you, I'll never take it off."

"I would like that." I smile at her, wanting to so desperately to kiss her lips, but I don't want to make her uncomfortable in front of her family.

"Are you in the States indefinitely, Trevor?" Dylan asks, pulling my gaze from Peggy.

I nod. "I'm home for good. I loved the work I've done, and I'm proud of being a part of an organization that helped so many people, but I think it's time to plant some roots, make a home, start a family. Besides, I'm next in line to run the family business."

"You did charity work, right?" Connor asks.

"It's a little more than that. We went where our services were needed the most. We went to areas where their living conditions were dire. A large group of us would travel there, willing to live among the people and help them build better lives for their families and community. Houses, medical centers, school, you name it, we made it happen. It was backbreaking work for sure."

"Peggy said you were a supervisor."

My attention goes to Clarisse. She's still nested in her husband's lap. "I was, but there was no office or desk work. The title basically means I made sure no one lost a limb and the work was kept on the proper timeline. I was just as much hands-on as the rest of the group."

Peggy places another piece of cake on my plate. She smiles at me and innocently sucks the chocolate from the pad of her finger, but it was the hottest thing I ever witnessed

"Excuse me," I say to her family, and lean over, taking her lips with mine. I couldn't help myself. "Thank you for the cake and those lips."

"Aw shit!, Y'all are sweeter than this damn ice tea," Rhonda grumbles.

Peggy's face is beet red.

"Rhonda, I think it's cute." The corners of Clarisse's lips tip up. Yeah, I'm not sure why Peggy was so nervous about this lunch.

∼

"Does Addie love her necklace?" Peggy asks as soon as I walk into her bedroom. She's laying on the bed.

I wanted her to come with me to tuck Adeline in, but she said that moment was just for Adeline and me. I get where she's coming from, but I don't want to leave Peggy out of anything in my life, especially when it involves Adeline. The only reason I didn't push the issue harder was because she said she would soak in a hot bath to help with her sore muscles.

I love being inside Peggy, but I hate that she's feeling discomfort. I'm a big man and Peggy's tight virgin hole wasn't ready for me. Even though her dropping down and taking me into her body was the best feeling in the world—and I can't wait to slide between her tight, velvety walls again—I wanted to ease her into it. I wanted to eat her out first, bring her to orgasm a few times, get her good and wet before I worked my cock inside her.

I'll give her a few days, and when I get her on her back and under me the way I want, I'll take her sweet pussy for hours and make her come until she begs me to stop. I've never felt a pussy like Peggy's, and I'm over the moon that hers is the only one I'll get for the rest of my life.

"Yes, she loved it. Her smile is so beautiful. She looks just like my mother—same eyes, nose, everything." I rub my chest to ease the ache there.

I've been feeling an overwhelming amount of love since walking through Peggy's door. The power behind it is something I have to get familiar with. I need to learn how to contain my feelings or I'm afraid my heart might burst. I've felt love before—for my mother, for my brother—but this love for Peggy and Adeline is so intense, it takes my breath away.

"She loves that you and she have the same one." I slip between her sheets and pull her close. Peggy is wearing another silky number, this one a dark green, and I'm guessing her pussy is bare underneath it. I want to side my hand up and feel if I'm correct, but giving her body some time will be impossible if I get one little feel of her wet cunt. To distract my mind from her nakedness, I say, "I have a company coming out tomorrow to install a security system in your house."

Peggy pulls back and gives me a look of shock. "You have what coming?"

"A security company. Look, you don't have an alarm system on this big house, and I need to know that you and Adeline are safe at all times. The thought that you were living alone here all these years with no protection makes me so mad, I want to lay you across my lap and spank your ass." I give her a quick swat on one ass cheek to stress my point.

Her eyes widen in surprise, and she blinks away her shock before she smiles and grinds her pussy against me. "Not really a punishment Mr. Duncan."

"Not a chance of sex tonight, angel. I'll let you get away with a lot, but not when your comfort is involved."

"But you're so hard," she whispers.

"I'm always hard when I'm around you. That's a given." I kiss her lips and reposition her body, pulling her against my chest. I have to distract her before she has me fucking her sore cunt. "So I was thinking a top tier system."

Peggy twists to look at me. "I never agreed to this alarm, Trevor. I've never wanted an alarm before because I don't need one. I'm safe on my property, and I've always felt safe here." She sits up and begin to tuck the covers around her body, as if she's drawing a line in the sand. Peggy values her independence and with her murderous glare, I'm being warned to tread carefully. She will plant her feet as deep as the roots in her garden if challenged.

"Baby, I know you feel safe and I would never want to make you uneasy. You live off the beaten path, you're miles from anyone, and an alarm will only provide extra protection."

"William has always been my extra protection, and I've been his."

"You are no longer William's concern!" I say louder and more forceful then I intend, but the thought of this guy with my angel gets under my skill and fucks with me in the worst way.

Oh shit. The heated scowl on Peggy's face is proof that William is the least of my concern. I reach for her hand and not only does she pull away from me, she slips from the bed and walks to the closed bedroom door.

"Get out." Peggy grabs the knob and swings the door open. "If you're going to take that tone with me…If you think this is acceptable…"

"I'm sorry. I didn't mean to raise my voice. I… I'm…"

"I need you to out of my room, Trevor." I make my way to her. I don't know how to explain that I'm riddled with jealousy and don't have the experience to know how to control it.

"What does William mean to you?"

"I…need…you…out!"

I stop where I am. I'm mere inches from Peggy, but the look in her eyes, that look of anger and fear, tells me I need to give her space. It tells me that I hit a trigger for her, and she's in protective mode. It tells me that I really fucked up, that I brought back feelings she experienced at the hands of a violent, sexual predator. A man she once trusted.

I nod my head and I walk past her, making sure I don't touch, mindful of her personal space. Once I'm in the hall, she quickly closes the door.

I stand in the hall, deciding what to do. I don't want to leave, not knowing the state of turmoil I put her in, so I sit on the floor in the hallway outside her room.

When she finally turns the lights off, I exhale and rest my head against her door. I sit there for several minutes before I head to my room.

I try to lay in bed, but I feel anxious not knowing what Peggy is thinking or feeling about me. I grab my laptop from the desk and decided to do some work. I log in to Braden's work email and begin to sort through some of the BS.

It's hard to concentrate, but I push through, because going back upstairs is not an option tonight, and I'll just toss and turn trying to sleep.

∼

I'M CONCENTRATING on the details of one of Braden's deals when I hear the faint whistle of the tea kettle. I walk toward the sound, out the bedroom door to the kitchen, telling myself I won't push her, I just want to see that she's okay.

In the doorway of the kitchen, I watch her standing at the stove with the hot kettle in her hand. I hold my breath. I'll wait until she acknowledges me. I don't wait long.

"William has never been anything more than a really good friend," Peggy starts with. Her back is to me while she's dunking her tea bag in the mug of hot water. I just listen. "After Clarisse left, I didn't have anyone. He's a good listener who sometimes takes me out to dinner so I don't always eat alone. He helps me with handy matters around the house."

"How long has he been building a life with you?" I might be digging a deeper hole for myself, but I need to know. If I ever want to deal with my jealousy, I need to know. "No man can be friends with a beautiful woman without catching feelings for her, especially you, angel."

Peggy shakes her head and turns to face me. She fists her hips and glares at me. "William and I have been friends for over six years, and he has not once been anything but respectful and decent with me."

"Okay… okay, I get it, angel. I get it. William was your uncomplicated companion, but does he know that he's been replaced?" I cross my arms and puff out my large chest, trying to mask my insecurities. I attempt a stern look while waiting for the words that will ease this ache and calm my green eyed monster. I may have failed. Peggy's fist drops from her hips and she begins to rock her sexy petite toes from tiptoes to heel and back again while she attempts to hide a smile. "Peggy." My tone warns that her silence isn't acceptable, and I'm still waiting. She tiptoe over until she's standing right in front of me and plants a soft kiss at the center of my chest before pulling my arms around her and snuggling into my body.

She doesn't say a word, but I know she understands that I can't help myself. I think it's because she had her own battle with her little green-eyed monster. I hold her close in an embrace. She continues to comfort me with warm kisses to my bare chest.

I whisper my apologies and bend to kiss her neck. She continues to wiggle and push upon my erection. I groan and thrust against her. I'm wearing another pair of basketball shorts, but this time without a shirt. I'm sure Peggy can feel my heart beating against her cheek. I'm trying to control myself, but this woman drives me crazy.

I grab her up and hold her while she wraps my waist with her sexy legs and grinds down on my hard body. "You need release, angel?"

"I need you, but you can't do this to me again, Trevor. You can't expect me to be ok with you wanting to control everything. I know your heart is in a good place regarding the security system, but you must always discuss concerns with me, when it's involving me. I had one man try to take away my right to choose what's best for me by threatening my safety." She holds my face with both hands and stares directly into my eyes. "I will never place myself in that situation again."

"I promise to never knowingly put you in that situation again. But full disclosure, I'm not perfect Peggy, I may misstep one day, and over the course of our years together, one day, may easily add up to many." She smiles at my honesty. "I ask that you promise to always communicate your feels, to help me get better at being the man you need."

"I promise." Her whispered words moisten my lips before she takes my mouth in a ravenous kiss.

In seconds, I have her nightshirt on the floor of her bedroom, her back pressed into the mattress, and her legs wide open with my face between her thighs. I latch on to her lips, loving her bare folds. Her back bows off the bed and I hold onto her hips. I will try not to exert my control over Peggy's life again, but her sexual pleasure is a whole other story. I want her under my control, at my mercy.

Peggy asked me for this, and when my angel asks, she receives. Her wants and needs will always rank top priority.

My mouth on Peggy's cunt, my tongue deep inside her folds, I feel like an animal marking his territory. I slide the flat of my tongue across her pussy then suck on her clit. She whispers my name repeatedly while I devour her, desperate for her nectar. Peggy tries to lift her hips to move against my mouth, and I allow her.

She works her center on me, and I know she's close. I thrust my tongue inside her, and she goes off. I drink every drop and bring her to orgasm twice before she's bone tired and completely sated. I kiss up her body, worshiping every inch, then settle between her legs and take her mouth, giving her a taste of herself.

"I love you, Trevor." She says it so sweetly my heart aches, and I pull her closer to me. I roll over, and she nestles into my chest.

That's where she remains until daylight creeps across my face. I slowly open my eyes, and the sexiest brown pair meets mine, accompanied with soft, pink lips. I sit up and take those lips. She moans and wiggles her nakedness on me.

"Good morning, angel."

"Good morning."

"What time is it?"

"It's early," she whispers and nibbles on my neck.

I groan and thrust my morning wood between her legs.

"Trevor," She breathes, and its music to my ears.

"What time does Adeline normally wake?" I'm not going to take Peggy, but I do want to give her greedy pussy a morning kiss.

"It's funny you ask. Normally she would be camped out under my bed. Was she there yesterday morning?"

"No, she called out to me from the doorway and asked for pancakes."

Peggy frowns and twists her full lips in thought.

"Is something wrong?" I ask.

"Maybe, but maybe not." She explains to me Adeline's habits from the last few months. "My first thought was that she was scared of the dark or just scared of being alone. I think with you here, she feels safe again."

I let her words sink in. I can't wait to get these business matters with Braden's open deals over and done with so I have the time to solidify this family with marriage, then adoption so Adeline can live in peace and always feel safe.

I roll Peggy on her back and hover over her. "Come on, let me give you a kiss before Adeline wakes."

She smiles and wraps her arms around my neck to pull me close, but I slip from her hold and slide down her body, kissing my way to her center.

8

PEGGY

"Peggy, can you just relax and enjoy the day? You're armed with an Amex Black Card and a worry-free afternoon. I was there when Trevor handed it over and told you to get what you and Addie need," Clarisse says.

We're shopping for Adeline and Riley in a boutique in town for our girls' vacation we planned during lunch yesterday. Clarisse and Dylan just finished renovations on a house near Myrtle Beach in South Carolina and in two weeks we'll be visiting for a full week stay. Riley and Adeline are trying on headbands, and Clarisse is looking through a rack of sundresses.

"I am having fun," I say, but the truth is, Trevor's Black Card is burning a hole in my pocketbook and not in the way one would think.

I've never had anyone take care of me. I've always made my own money. When my mom traveled with me, I paid her a manager's percentage because she'd put her life on hold to make sure I lived out my dream. I loved my mother for all she did for me, but I also felt crappy for taking her away from Clarisse. I guess I felt better that I was able to pay her for the sacrifices she freely made for me. But what's really bothering me is that he assumed I would spend his money on me as though I've earned the right to do so.

Trevor and I are in love, there's no questioning that. I want to spend the rest of my life with him, and he wants the same from me. Which is why I decided to compromise with the alarm system. I feel I don't need it, but what harm will it do to have one? I feel fine giving him that one request. Going back to his money—he has an obligation to take care of Adeline and all her purchases are on his card, but I have a right to choose what I do and don't do involving Trevor, and I want to keep it that way. I've been around powerful men wrapped up in their millions for most of my life, and I've seen firsthand how they use their money to control women and treat them as if they are property.

I don't think Trevor is trying to control me with his money, but I want us to be on an equal playing field, if only for my comfort. I didn't have a chance to discuss my concerns with him before taking the card, but we'll be home soon enough and I'll explain my stance to him. I'm sure he'll understand.

"Are we dressing as twins for the week away in Myrtle Beach?" Clarisse asks, pulling me from my thoughts.

"No! You would never catch me in some of the outfits you wear," I say.

"The hell does that mean? I know how to dress—"

I cut her off, laughing, before she could curse at me. "I'm kidding, I'm kidding. I know you were talking to the girls. You should have seen your face. I think the whites of your eyes even turned red."

I can't stop laughing at her expression. Because of her pregnancy, Clarisse and her emotions are all over the place. I know I shouldn't tease her, because she could start crying any minute, which will set Riley off and Dylan will get pissed. "Sorry, Clari. I was only teasing. You're very beautiful."

She gives me a side-eye before she giggles.

"What are we doing, girls, yellow or pink?" I call to Adeline and Riley. As I expect, they decide on both.

"Is that all?" I ask Trevor regarding my new security system, after placing our shopping bags upstairs. He told me he was securing the downstairs doors and a few windows upstairs. Now I'm looking at a four-way split-screen monitor on the kitchen counter with the entire perimeter of my house on display.

"Yes, but the great thing about this system is you can download the app onto your cell phone and view a live feed, as well as rewind the footage, anywhere and anytime. The system also has motion detectors and will alert you if someone rings your bell or breaks the glass on the windows or doors."

I can't help the smile that splits my lips. I should be angry. I should be extremely fucking pissed off, because one, he took the liberty of making decisions without consulting me first, and second, he paid the tab for the monthly monitoring. Lastly, he's showing me all these super cool features from *his* cell phone. Yes, I should be livid, but he's smiling so wide and his eyes are bright with excitement. I can't find it in me to even frown.

"I thought it would be good…" His expression turns sheepish, and he looks at the feed on his phone. "That I have the app too. There are several projects involving the casino that will take me to Vegas, possibly weeks at a time. I'll work from home on as much as I can, but I will have to travel there soon. Plus, with you and Adeline being away a week with your sister, it'll make me breathe a little easier if I know we can monitor the house."

He turns those sexy-ass hazel eyes on me, and my insides melt. Oh my, this man makes me feel like doing some dirty, dirty things to him, things I've only read about. He smiles and takes my lips with his in a quick kiss. I'm sure it's a thank you for not fighting him on the alarm. He could get me to do damn near anything he suggests, but right now, I want him to suggest putting his cock between my legs. He takes me in his arms, and I go willingly. I'm happy Clarisse offered to take the kids to the movies after our shopping, because it's been a few days, and I want him inside me.

"There's also night vision," he whispers. He kisses my collarbone. "I know how you love to relax outside on the patio." He moves his lips up my neck, causing a shiver down my spine. "If you happen to decide to enjoy moon bathing, let's say in nothing but this"—he takes the charm on my necklace—"that would be appreciated, too."

He nuzzles me and I moan.

"How was shopping?" He pulls away from me and I want to scream. "I should have asked earlier, but I assumed it went well, considering the amount of bags hauled upstairs."

"Yeah, well, shopping was good. I got Adeline quite a few outfits, because you'll never believe the amount of messes kids get into on vacation." I can't wait to vacation with him and Adeline soon.

"Have you and Adeline vacationed before?"

"Yes, a small one. We went to the beach, then this large farmer's market, and pigged out on fresh fruit and junk food. Adeline ate too much, and I had to give her Pepto before bed, or as Adeline calls them, 'the pink candy.'"

"What about you? Were you able to find some outfits for you?"

"About that… I did find a few things too, but I didn't use your card for them."

"Why not?"

"I didn't believe it was right for me to charge my purchases to your card." I grab two beers from the fridge and set them on the island, sliding one to him.

"Okay."

"Okay?" I repeat.

"Yeah, I get it. We've only known each other a hot minute. I can see how it would be uncomfortable for me to throw my money in your face. I'm sorry for making you feel like *that* type of woman."

"And what type of woman would I have been if I had used your card?" I ask, not holding back my frown.

He shrugs before grabbing the neck of his bottle and twisting the cap. He takes a sip and sits on the barstool.

I'm getting impatient. "Waiting."

"The woman who can tell when someone is repaying her for

room and board, for continuing to help care for a little girl who is clearly not her responsibility any longer. I assumed you could see that I would never hold anything over your head or use the money I happen to have against you." He takes another swig from his bottle, emptying it this time. "I saw your expression when I insisted you take the card. I'm not trying to control your life, Peggy. My mother set up a trust fund, one that I've never touched, when she was first diagnosed with cancer. She didn't trust my father to ensure our care, and she wanted us to be financially stable. Thanks to her forethought and an excellent investment firm, I'm a billionaire even without the casino. But the man I'm offering you is a simple man, who has always lived his life chasing the next adventure and running from any real responsibility. One look at you, and all I desire is to be anywhere you are. We may have only known each other a short while, but I know you. I'd rather spoil you with love, time, and attention, not with a few outfits and material BS you're more than capable of providing for yourself."

He stands from the barstool and grips my chin. His eyes search mine before he kisses away the stupid expression I know is on my face.

I slide my hands under his T-shirt and over his back and abs. The hard bulge of his cock digs into my stomach. He moans, giving me a rush of arousal. My hands slide from his waist into the back of his jeans, giving his cheeks a squeeze while I rub up against him. "I want you."

"Oh, angel, I want you more than you know, but your body needs some time. You're sore, and I don't want to hurt you."

"Baby, you can't hurt me unless you leave me. That'll break my heart."

He smiles and gives me one more kiss before stepping out of my grip. I'm aching so intensely, I want to scream. I step closer and grab his cock, marveling in the feel of him, so hard.

I lick my lips before I tiptoe and lick the base of his neck. "Please, Trevor."

Before I know what's happening, he has me face down with my

cheek pressed to the cool granite counter top of the island. I feel him gather the material of my long maxi dress up around my waist, exposing my gray lace panties. He grabs my hands, locking them at the wrist, holding them above my head on the counter. He massages my lips through my panties. I'm so wet and getting wetter at each stroke.

"Please, Trevor."

"I'll give you relief, angel, but I'm not fucking you right now." He drops to his knees and places a kiss on both of my ass cheeks. One at a time he spreads my legs farther apart so he can kiss my female lips through my wet panties before he moves the material aside and latches onto my clit. I cry out as he growls against my tender flesh. He devours me, bringing me to orgasm in no time. My legs tremble and I gasp, one hand grabbing the edge of the counter. He grips my ass and presses my center against his mouth while he takes my orgasm from me.

After my release, I'm bone-tired and light-headed. He lifts me into his arms and carries me to his room, where he places me on his bed. I'm too tired to do anything but watch him plant his ass in the office chair at the desk under the window, where he opens his laptop.

He sits there doing some work while I'm being lulled to sleep, listening to the tapping of the keys on his laptop, thinking, *Damn, I can't wait to be fucked by this man.*

9

TREVOR

It's no surprise that I love kissing Peggy between her legs. Her lips are sweet and smooth, and the feel of my tongue sliding between her folds is heavenly. They quiver and grip my tongue, pulling me inside. I tease her opening with the tip of my tongue, playfully torturing her, increasing her pleasure, before I wrap my lips around her clit, sucking and gently pulling her pleasure to the forefront. Her long fingers thread through my dreads, kneading and rubbing my scalp, urging me on. I want to bring her to the brink of pleasure before I slide between her juicy lips.

"Trevor, oh baby, I'm so close." She moans and arches her back, pushing her clit against my mouth.

I release her lower lips and kissing them once more. After positioning the head of my cock at her tight entrance, I thrust in. She groans and her back bows. The pleasure of her squeeze on my thickness is so intense, I shut my eyes and take a deep breath to steady my pulsing heart. I growl from the squeeze on my cock and my heart at once.

"Shit," I grunt through clenched teeth. The sound of my voice is unfamiliar, and I blink, attempting to adjust to the emotions at war inside me.

I thrust in and out of her, slowly increasing my speed. She moans my name and I swoop in and take her mouth to silence her, because if I hear that sexy rasp in her voice coating every syllable of my name, I'm going to fuck her sinfully delicious pussy without control. I release her mouth and puff out a breath, feeling my chest relax when the clenching of her walls eases as she comes down from what felt like an extremely intense orgasm.

"More. Please don't stop now."

"Never, angel. The best place to be is inside this tight cunt. I want you to come on my cock again, baby, before I fill your body with my seed."

"Oh, I love you. Fuck! You're so big. Give me your cum, baby. I want every last drop of your essence." She's topping from the bottom, knowing how to make me give her what she wants. Her words spoken in that sexy-as-fuck rasp her voice gets after she orgasms always does me in.

"Oh shit, angel."

"Fill me up." She swivels her hips, meeting each thrust with equal force.

I growl and grab her hips, locking them under me. I cage her with a hand on either side of her head, pressing down on her pelvic bone. The movement repositions my cock, and I have direct contact with her sweet spot while applying friction to her clit.

"I want your pleasure, angel, you will not deny me what I want." I take her bottom lip between my teeth and pull her plump flesh, sucking it into my mouth. "Your body belongs to me, from every quiver of arousal, to your hard nipples begging for my mouth, my tongue. When your cunt is dipping and hot, it will only release when I say, and I'm calling for my sweet, obedient, tight little cunt to wet my cock."

"Oh, shit. Yes."

Her core squeezes my cock, pulsing, milking me hard. I continue to ride her G-spot, grunting out my release and shooting cum inside her unprotected womb.

"I don't want to go." She whispers her protest to their girls week in South Carolina. "Two weeks have gone by fast and you've spoiled me. I don't want to be without you."

"Angel, you never will be." I roll over and take her with me, my cock embedded deep inside her body. I plan to keep it there until we have to get up and face our day. I wrap my arms around her body and hold her so close I can feel her heart beating against my chest. She snuggles into my chest, nuzzles my chin, and kisses my lips, creating that familiar ache in my heart.

I grab her face and deepen the kiss. The slide of her tongue in my mouth and the pull of her soft, full lips on mine have my hips thrusting into her center slowly, loving on Peggy.

∽

"I'VE MADE progress on the merger, but the Spencers want to re-negotiate previous terms left unresolved. Braden was working on them before…be…fore."

"I get it Jennifer."

Loud gulps from whatever beverage my brother's executive assistant is drinking come down the line, then ice clinking in a glass. "What have you been doing in the meantime to appease them until I'm able to evaluate other options?" I ask.

"I'm waiting for Mr. Spencer's son to contact me, but I've laid out several of the usual alternatives Braden would normally offer up. I've come up empty-handed with each one."

I'm pacing the guest room I've been using as my office for the last two week since my clothes are now rooming with Peggy's clothes in her closet. I'm anxious because I don't want to drag this out any longer than needed. I have a life to start.

"Well, Mr. Duncan, I wish it was easier to close this one, but sometimes we have to play hardball."

Since my brother's death, I've learned he was dabbling in all sorts of "businesses," and he negotiated more in the bedroom then in the boardroom. Not only did he run the casino, he also ran girls, and I've heard he may have had some dealings with the mob.

This deal with Jericho Spencer is the only arrangement with any real substance. Braden was the only point of contact with the other two open contracts, and since he was no longer with us, they pulled out—which I didn't mind. Probably shady anyway. The plan is to merge with Spencer's Paradise, a high-end spa which neighbors The Golden Temple. Being one of the largest spas on the strip, the merger will be lucrative for The Golden Temple casino for sure.

Annoyed, I roll my neck as I leave the room after ending the call with Jennifer, giving her the task to find out the terms Jericho and his father want to address. I spent most of my time laying out my department audits. I need to first clean house and rid the place of all this fuckery before I finalize any mergers.

It's the eve of Peggy and Adeline's trip to South Carolina with Clarisse and Riley, and I want to cook for them. I persuaded the girls to go and spend the afternoon at Adeline's favorite ice cream shop for a cone, and I would have dinner ready when they returned, but thanks to this bullshit, with the casino and this merger I'm late. Peggy and Adeline returned home two hours ago. She peeked in on me, blew a kiss, and disappeared down the hallway.

"Hi, Uncle Trevor." Adeline pops up from the end of the stairs. She's all smiles and my spirits brighten. "Look, I'm wearing my hair bow today, Uncle Trevor. See? It matches my sundress." She's wearing a red dress adorned with daisies. Her headband matches perfectly, and she looks adorable.

"You look beautiful, little bird." I scoop her up and deposit her on the barstool so we can talk while I cook. Her smile fades into a frown. I realize, she's used to me calling her Adeline, but I'm the only person who addresses her so formally. I don't have a pet name for her. Peggy calls her squirt, and everyone else calls her Addie.

"Why you call me that? Am I a little bird like my necklace? Does that mean you love me as much as you love Peggy? She's your angel and now I'm your little bird?"

I put down the knife, flatten my palms on the island, and lean over so I'm eye level to Adeline before I say, "I've always loved you. I've loved you since the day your father told me I had a niece." She smiles, and so do I. "When I received word that you were born, I was so happy for my brother, for our family, because you are our mother's first grandchild. Your father named you after our mother, and I've always felt connected to you. Do you think a person's heart can split in two?"

She gives my question careful consideration. "No. They would die. Their heart would be broken and stop working." She looks sad.

I feel a little shitty for asking, so I quickly say, "Their heart splits in two, but not physically. I mean the love that comes from their heart goes in two directions. My heart is split between you and Peggy."

Adeline brightens up my day with that smile. "I want to tell William that I'm your little bird. I heard him tell Peggy at the ice cream shop that she's important to you. I'm important too."

My bright day becomes overcast with a red haze. I spoke with Peggy while they were at the ice cream shop and she never said anything about William being with them.

I try on a smile for Adeline's sake. "Where is Peggy?"

"She's packing for the beach."

I'm scooping Adeline up once again and take the stairs two at a time. When I make it to the landing I instruct her to play until dinner. She skips to the playroom down the hall from her bedroom. When she disappears into the room, I quickly walk to our room.

I stand in the doorway and watch Peggy's sexy ass bouncing in tight shorts as she forces a large suitcase closed. My mouth waters and my teeth ache to feel the soft flesh of her cheeks after I finish enjoying her pussy. I force myself to remember why I searched her out in the first place.

"Hi, angel, how's packing? How much do you have left to do?"

I attempt to calm the fire raging inside me, and I want to hear her voice, soft and relaxed, before I piss her off. I'm only half listening to her while I work on talking myself out of hopping into her ATV and trucking over to Williams place and demanding he back off. I'm being irrational, but she's my angel, and until I have her tied to me forever, this crazy inside me may never ease.

She asks me a question, but I don't hear it. Instead of asking her to repeat it, I go directly to the problem. "Why did Adeline tell me about ice cream with William?"

"Trevor…" She has the audacity to sound exasperated.

Fuck that! "Why wouldn't you say something to me?"

Her eyes turn soft and pleading. She walks past my tense body to close her door.

"Do you care that I'm upset?" I ask.

She sighs. "I do care that you're upset because that means we have a bigger problem than I thought. Now let's get this straight— William is my next-door neighbor, and my very good friend, and you will never get to forbid me to talk to my friend without just cause. William has done nothing wrong, Trevor. He's been nice to Adeline since she got here. He built her playground set out back and hung all the shelves in her room to hold all her keepsakes. He knows my feelings for you. He told me he could see that you were in love with me."

"When in the hell did he see that? He never took his eyes off you."

"William is not the problem here, Trevor. It's your attitude, your jealousy." She crosses her arms over her chest and closes her eyes. I believe she's calming her anger toward me. She opens her eyes. "Baby, I love you," she says, but her voice doesn't soften like it usually does, and a stab of concern pierces my heart. "I'm yours, and I will always be yours. But this intense display from you has me wondering if you truly believe me when I say those words. Do you really distrust William, or do you doubt me?"

After she asks her question, I realize that she's not angry, but she's hurting. I rush to her, and to my surprise she doesn't pull away from me. She allows me to hold her. She's right. My jealousy is getting out of hand, but it has nothing to do with her. I don't doubt Peggy, and I'm the biggest jackass for giving her any reason to think that I do.

"I love you, angel."

She wraps her arms tightly around me as I'm holding onto her. I repeat the words and pray she believes me. I press my lips to her forehead, her cheeks, and finally I taste her lips, whispering my love for her across them before taking them in a deeper, longer connection.

When I pull away, I rest my forehead onto hers and palm her cheeks to hold her in place. I want to stare into her brown eyes when I give her my truth. "You're right, my jealousy is a problem. I don't doubt you, I know you love me. Angel, you are everything, my world, my heart, and I only just found you."

"Trevor, please don't allow your jealousy to destroy us because William is my friend and he will always be my friend. You are my future, my world, it's just you and me, baby."

I take her into my arms again and hold her longer. I need to control my caveman antics, because losing her is not an option. I slide my hands inside her shorts and grope the soft warm flesh of her ass.

"Trevor, I still have so much to do to get ready." She attempts to protest but pushes her ass into my hands and moans. I take her mouth, needing to taste her before I let her finish her packing.

"We'll have time tonight." I take one last taste from her before I pull away.

I peek in on Adeline before I head downstairs and ask if she would help me with dinner. I tell her I want to spend some time with my little bird before they leave.

～

I'VE BEEN in Vegas for nearly three weeks cleaning house. My department audit has been grueling. I can't believe the types of shit Braden was allowing. I've had to threaten to press charges on more than a few former employees. At this rate I'll have to go through an even grueling hiring process to recoup our dwindling staff. I've been dying a slow death every day without my angel. My plan was to only be gone the week Peggy and Adeline were away on vacation. I left for Vegas the same day they left for Myrtle Beach but took a later flight so I could see them off.

After the first two days I knew this audit was going to be hell, adding an extra two weeks to my stay. I received a call from Mr. Spencer, informing me that he's ready to talk terms, but I have yet to receive his counter in writing.

"Trevor, we can run down the details face to face."

"Mr. Spencer, I look forward to our meeting, seeing as we're both eager to make money together, but not until I have the counter to our terms in writing. You can email them to Jennifer and I'll be in contact thereafter."

This is my last attempt at finalizing this business arrangement. After the dust settles, I don't need to be as hands on with the casino. I'll only need to travel to Vegas maybe one week each month, and let the executives that remain run the show.

But right now, I can't remain in Vegas another fucking day, away from my angel and little bird. I've been talking to Peggy via FaceTime since I arrived weeks ago. She's asked questions about the business and even shared some incite of her own. She's been encouraging, and its meant the world to me to have someone in my corner.

Since I've been gone, Peggy's enrolled Adeline in a summer art program and ballet classes. She has Adeline on more of a schedule now that her living arrangements are more stable, and from what she tells me, Adeline loves it. I know Peggy loves it too. I see the gleam in her eyes every evening we FaceTime. She always has a different story of something funny or cute Adeline has done. I enjoy watching her prepare dinner with her hair pulled up in a pineapple or a tight knot atop her head. With her iPhone on the holder, I can admire the sway of her hips, the bounce of her lush ass clad in yoga shorts or a thin maxi skirt while she mixes, stirs, and chops. It's just as enjoyable as seeing her naked and spread out on her bed.

Before I address my meeting with Mr. Spencer with Jennifer, I FaceTime Peggy. It's late in Georgia and I want to catch her before she falls to sleep.

"All the windows and doors locked?" I ask when I see she's already in bed.

"Check."

"The alarm set?" I follow my usual safety checklist with her.

"Check."

"You looked over the monitors before heading up to bed?"

"Check." She answers with obvious annoyance.

"What about—"

"Check, check, and check. Trevor, we go through this every night. Adeline and I are safe behind these walls. Adeline is sleeping. She has an early morning at the civic center."

"Right, her field trip! Is she excited? Are you going with them to the art museum?"

"Yes, she is excited, but… umm, no, I have a thing in the morning." Peggy looks away from the screen briefly and rubs the back of her neck.

Peggy and I have been together a little over two months, and it took me half that time to recognize her tells. When Peggy is holding back or uncomfortable, she fidgets and avoids eye contact.

"A thing?" I ask.

"Yeah, an appointment."

"What kind of appointment?"

She sighs. "Like, an annual thing at the doctor's."

"Doctor? Peggy, you're not feeling well?"

She nods. "It's just a checkup. I figured her field trip was the best time for it. Adeline has all her appointments scheduled for next month, before she begins first grade."

"Right, first grade. Do you think she'll enjoy going to school with the twins?"

"Absolutely. They're so close now. I can only imagine how close they'll become once they see each other daily." As she talks, she slips out of her nightshirt and climbs under the covers.

"Long day, angel?" I ask, noticing she's a little sluggish this evening.

Though her eyes still hold her usual gleam of happiness, they now show exhaustion. She shrugs and rests her head on her pillows.

I palm my chest, longing to be by her side. "I love you, Peggy."

She smiles so sweetly and her eyelids flutter closed before lazily opening.

"I miss you, angel. I hate this shit. I just want this over and done so I can be with you."

"I love you, Trevor. I want you with me too, especially right now, tomorrow, the day after, the weeks after, the months and years to come. I thought I enjoyed being alone, that I was happy with the peace and silence, but that was only because I didn't have you or Adeline. Now I'm so sad when I'm alone." Her eyes sparkle with tears, and my heart breaks even more.

"Peggy, baby, please don't be sad. I have to wrap up the last few details before I can catch the next flight out and be there in a few hours," I say. I push up from the sofa in the owner's suite and make my way to the laptop.

"No, no, you don't have to rush back. Finish your business there. I'm just feeling a little out of sorts right now. I'll be fine, I promise." She attempts a smile but only breaks down.

I want to burn this casino to the ground.

"I don't understand, what's wrong with me today. This isn't the first time I've cried for nothing. This morning it was a burnt pancake." The tears pooling on her pillow break my heart.

She sighs. "Don't worry about it. I don't mean to add extra stress on you. I told you, I never had this before, so I'm a little selfish with you."

"Angel, if I had a choice, I wouldn't be here now. I would have been with you three weeks ago, but I can't avoid this, but I promise it'll get better. I can't wait until I get it done, because I'll never have to leave your side again."

She wipes the tears from her cheeks, and I die a little more inside.

"Angel, I've booked a flight out for the morning."

"I miss you holding me."

I search her red eyes, and a twinge of panic shoots through my veins, chilling my blood. "Is something the matter, something more than what you're telling me?"

She stares at me, and I can feel she has so much on her mind. I can see her indecision playing out in her sad eyes.

"Angel, you're killing me baby. I'm too far away to make this better, to make you feel better. I need you to give me something, sweetheart. Not knowing will drive me insane."

"Just make it when you can."

"Peggy—"

"Trevor, please, I'm so tired and I'm missing you like crazy." Her words are full of emotion.

My body is flooded with defeat, and I feel helpless. She must have placed the holder on her dresser, because she turns on her back and stares at the ceiling and I can only see her profile. I want her eyes back on me, but I can't stand the look they were giving me, so I settle for my defeat and allow her rest. I'll be with her tomorrow, and we can sort this all out then.

"I'm leaving first thing in the morning, angel."

"Okay."

I watch her until she falls asleep, neither of us saying another word. When she's out for the night, I end the FaceTime and toss my phone on the bed. I reach for the hotel phone to arrange for a car to take me to the airport in the morning.

10

PEGGY

Adeline is now at Clarisse's house, and I'm on my way into town to shop for a few things. Trevor should be in the air by now. I was expecting him earlier this morning, but he missed the flight. He said it was an emergency involving one of the casino employees.

I didn't give him any attitude about it. He has a lot to deal with and has shared with me the issues he's encountered while cleaning house, on top of the merger. I really want to help him, but I don't know the first thing about the casino business, but I do know my man. I want to really make his home-coming special.

He inquired about my doctor's appointment this morning, but I don't have anything to share. It really was just a checkup.

This is the first time Trevor and I have been apart longer then a few hours, and I've been going crazy. I had to keep myself and Adeline busy, so I searched out every available summer program I could sign her up to attend.

I'm happy Clarisse offered to host a sleepover weekend, because what I have planned for my handsome, sexy man is a night of pure pleasure and sinful seduction. My goal is to make him scream my name.

I've only ever seduced a man while in front of a camera and

surrounded by hair and makeup, assistants, set crew, and photographers shouting, "Give me sexy, give me seduction." It was pretend, all of it, and I'm great at that. I can morph into who I need to be. Simply by changing my hair, clothes, makeup, Peggy Jordan fades into the background.

I'm skilled at pretend, but that's not who and what I am with Trevor. I remind myself again that I can shed these layers of skepticism, apprehension, and protection and allow Peggy to exist as her quirky, carefree, romantic self. I can do this only with Trevor.

At a lingerie shop, I buy a few items. Less than ten minutes after I get there, the salesperson is trying her hardest to sell me the most obnoxious pieces in the store, but I'm still Trevor's angel, so I take that as inspiration while I roam. When I make it to the register, I have several possibilities in my hands.

"You wouldn't like a fitting room?" the salesperson asks, holding up my articles of clothing. I use the words loosely.

"No, I don't need a room. I know they'll fit." I just want to make my purchase, toss these bad boys in a gentle wash, and hang them in my laundry room while I hope at least one dries before Trevor walks through my door.

She wraps my last item in paper, giving me a once-over before handing me my bags. "Have a good day."

With a polite smile, I turn and leave. I rush to my car and make my way home.

∽

"Peggy, you need to shake this." I stand in my walk-in closet in front of my floor-length mirror, staring at my reflection. It's late, after eleven in the evening, and Trevor's flight landed about twenty minutes ago. I suspect it'll take him an additional forty-five minutes to get home. "You're hot. You're going to blow his dreads back when he gets a look at you in this outfit. Well... maybe outfit isn't an accurate description."

I turn and check out my barely covered ass in the softest, pink lace booty short panties. I've always been rather thin, but I have a graciously lush ass with curvy hips. My mother blessed me with what some have referred to as the perfect female frame, a perfect hourglass. I wiggle my ass a little and can't help but agree.

"You are going to kill that man so good." I laugh and shake my head at the ridiculous conversation I'm having with my reflection. I face the mirror and smooth my bone-straight hair over my shoulders. It drapes over my bare breasts, and the ends kiss the top of my hips. I rest my right palm over my bluebird charm and take a breath. "Stop worrying, he'll love it."

I leave the closet and head downstairs. It took me the entire afternoon to slip on a pair of panties. You'd think I was going to a fancy ball, complete with glass slippers and a floor-length gown.

After a shower, where I washed and conditioned my hair with my favorite products, I spent most of the day blow-drying, flat-ironing, and styling it. I barely had time to apply a coat of red polish on my toenails. Now I'm walking carefully, trying not to smudge them while I check on dinner in the oven. I prepared a spinach quiche before I showered, and it's been in the warmer. I also have a small salad in the chiller and a nice bottle of pinot grigio. For dessert, I have two cans of whipped topping, ambition, and an eagerness to please.

I hear what sounds like a car door and check the four-way monitor. Trevor has arrived sooner than I expected. My stomach drops, and I panic. I rush from one room to the next, trying to find the perfect place to present him with his welcome home gift. I stand in front of the door so I'm the first thing he sees, then I think better of myself. I rush to the family room, lounge in a sexy pose on the sofa, and think not. I worked too hard for him not to see all this ass—not to mention my hair is a big part of my "outfit."

With my ass still on my mind and—dare I say—how hot I looked in the mirror, I decide to greet him in the kitchen and serve him his dinner in all my naked glory. I pull the salad from the fridge and place it on the island. I stare at the monitor and watch my big man crawl at a snail's pace up the stairs. He looks dead tired, and a stab of guilt hits me. He's going to take one look at me and know exactly what I want, and he'll push through his exhaustion so as not to disappoint me.

I look around for something to cover my nakedness but I'm out of time. I hear the system beep as Trevor disarms Stay Mode on the alarm. For reasons unknown to me, I have a strong urge to cry. My emotions have been all haywire lately. I turn my back to the kitchen door, trying to school my emotions before I greet him.

"Holy shit."

I turn slowly to face him. My eyes are brimming with unshed tears, and I'm frozen in place by the heated look in his eyes. Trevor is wearing a pair of cargo shorts and a white T-shirt. His dreads are loose and framing his gorgeous face, and I swear he's as sexy now as he is in just a pair of boxers.

I'm speechless as he moves toward me. The swagger in his walk, the undeniable confidence in the way he sets his broad shoulders, has my body heating, reminding me of how my body reacted when he first walked through my kitchen doors.

Before I know it, he's standing right in front of me, licks his bottom lip, and my insides melt. I'm so hot that if a gust of cold air were to pass over my naked skin, steam would rise off me. Trevor dwarfs me as usual. I stare into his eyes, and a shiver shoots up my spine and my lips part. My breath dries my lips, and I have to lick them, forcing his eyes to my mouth.

I can't speak, and tears are still hanging on my lids. I scan his face, taking in every inch of it. Damn, I missed him!

His soft lips are framed by a thin goatee and the patch of hair that covers his chin contains a dusting of gray mixed in with his light brown. The beauty of his golden brown complexion and light hazel eyes always puts me in a daze for a minute or two. I feel naked under his gaze. Not just physically naked, but soul naked, so exposed. The feeling is intoxicating, addictive, and wetness pools on the crotch of my panties.

Behind his stare is a smidge of exhaustion, and I'm struggling to do the right thing, which is feeding him and allowing him to rest. On the other hand, I want to drop to my knees, take his massive cock from his shorts, and worship it with my mouth, hands, and the warmth between my breast and my legs.

The urge to be selfish is winning. I'm so aware of how weak he makes me, and the killer part of it is that I don't give a flying fuck. I want to submit and dominate at the same time. I want to scream at him to touch me, yet I crave the feeling of surrender. Trevor has yet to touch me and I can't move—not until he tells me to.

His gaze roams the front of my body, down to my red-painted toenails and back to the charm nesting between my breasts. He lifts his hand, and I gasp at the feathery-light graze of his fingers when he touches the charm. I can't pull my eyes from his to see what he's doing. His hazel gaze is hypnotic. When I feel his fingers gently pull at my hard nipples, I know they've poked through the veil of hair I draped over them. Arousal hits me right in the gut and I stop breathing—until my tears break free and slide down my flushed cheeks.

"Angel."

His whisper brings more tears to the surface, and they spill over.

He steps closer, presses his chest against mine, and slides his large hands down my waist and around my hips to cuff my lace-covered ass. "Legs, angel."

I go weak into his strong arms and wrap my legs around his waist, wrapped in his soft lavender scent. His dreads tickle my cheeks and my neck as I hold on. The scrape of the chair legs on my floor has me looking through the window behind the kitchen table, where I see the reflection of his wide back laced with my long legs and arms. He sits down with me, and I drop my legs, allowing them to dangle at his side. "I know what you need. After I give it to you, then I want us to talk."

I still can't speak. All I can do is nod like an obedient child, and I feel no shame from it either. I want him to lead me, to dominate me, and make my body react. He fingers my hair off my breasts to expose my nipples. He palms my breasts, and his thumbs slowly circle my areolas. The pleasure is so intense, I close my eyes and struggle not to come.

"Keep those eyes open, angel, keep them on me. I don't want you to look away."

I do as I'm told and catch his gaze, trying not to melt into his touch. His hand slides into the front of my panties, and the first touch of his finger on my clit has me teetering on the edge.

"Angel, you are close, baby. I can feel how desperate your tight center is, how needy." He kisses my neck and moves to my jaw, then the tip of my chin. "I'm going to kiss your lips now, angel. I don't want you to kiss me back until I slip my tongue into your mouth."

I feel the invasion of his fingers into my body at the same time he takes my lips. He slowly finger fucks me, softly pulling at my lips. He whispers dirty words between kisses while increasing his thrusts. Trevor is driving me insane and I want to scream and cry, but my arousal has me paralyzed. I feel the tight pull from deep inside my core and I have to hold my breath not to climax, but I'm stunned when Trevor nips my bottom lip.

"Obey, angel," he growls, and I relax against him and let go.

When I do, he slips his tongue between my lips. I greedily take his mouth as a muffled scream rips me in half and I orgasm around his fingers. The pull in my core is so strong, I swear I black out. When he finally ends the kiss, pulling away from me, I feel dizzy and cold. I slouch against his chest and close my eyes as my head spins. He removes his fingers from my body and inserts them into his mouth, and I shiver. The quivers are so deep inside me, if not for his arms engulfing me, I would have seized from panic.

Once I'm warm and cozy in his arms and on his lap, he says, "I will always take care of you, angel. Your needs are priority. Never forget that."

I nod and kiss his neck.

"I love the outfit," he says with a smile in his words.

I giggle and nuzzle his neck. "I'm so happy you like it. You have no idea how stressful slipping on a pair of lace panties really is."

"I think I have an idea. I could see the stress creeping up your body." He plants a kiss on my forehead, and I smile, the most relaxed I've felt in three weeks. "What's with the salad and wine?"

"I made you a light late-night dinner. I didn't want you going to bed hungry, and I'm sure you haven't eating anything decent all day." I look up at him. "I have a quiche in the oven." I take his lips with mine, and the taste of me on his tongue has my body heating up again. I wiggle and grind on his lap.

He pulls away and lifts me right off his lap and onto wobbly legs. "You cooked, baby. We'll eat first, then I'll fuck you anywhere and everywhere you want me."

I swear my ovaries did a complete somersault. The man has my body humming with electrical energy just from the thought of being with him. I turn toward the stove, and he slaps my ass before pulling me back to him and planting a kiss to the small of my back.

∼

"I love watching you work, angel."

The gruff tone of his voice makes me excited and full of pride that I'm responsible for the noises he makes. Trevor finally let me have full control over his sexual pleasure, and tasting him as he's tasted me so many times was first on my to-do list. I've never experienced anything sexual before Trevor. His kisses are heavenly, his cock is delicious, and I think I'm getting just as addicted to blowing him as I'm to him bringing me to orgasm.

"Careful, angel, I'm close."

The pure agony in his words sparks the minx in me to push forward. My effort increases, wanting him to finish while in my mouth. I want to feel the pulse of his cock between my lips while he grips my hair, ruining hours of hard work.

"Angel…" he says with warning.

I lift my gaze to meet his and deep throat his cock. I wasn't aware of how controlled my gag reflex is until now. Keeping my eyes connected with his, I swallow around his thickness, giving him a tight squeeze. He growls my name, which he rarely uses anymore. He palms my face, holding my head still, then the first burst of his release hits the back of my throat and I swallow. I drink him down to the last drop before licking his tip clean.

"Is your mouth where I'm supposed to come, angel?" Trevor asks. The frown that adorns his beautiful face does nothing to hide how his hazel eyes are brighter after his orgasm.

I don't speak, only shake my head and bite my bottom lip, attempting to hide my triumphant smirk.

"I told you, I only release inside this sexy body." He hoists me up so we are eye to eye, nose to nose.

His thick cock slips between my folds, still solid as if he didn't just shoot cum down my throat. I moan my pleasure and ride him hard and fast, not wanting to relinquish my control, because who knows when he'll let me have it again after the stunt I just pulled. In no time, my muscles tighten along with my core, stilling my movements. My shoulders lock up to my neck, my head falls forward, pressing my forehead against his, and the sounds I make fill the room, deafening me. I can't hear the words he's speaking, but I feel the slight puffs of his breath playing across my lips and neck.

When I come back from my orgasmic experience, Trevor's pulsing cock unloads deep inside my body. I place kisses across his forehead as he grunts out his release, and the sound shoots straight to my center where we're still connected. I slowly swirl my hips.

"You are really trying to kill me, woman."

"No, not at all, I love you too much. I just can't get enough of you." I swirl my hips again, he thrusts once more, and before I know it, I'm on my back with Trevor looking down at me.

"I think you've had enough, angel. Handing over control to you? I see now that puts you on this crazy insatiable power trip."

He kisses my pouty lips. "You like it better when I'm in control anyway, don't you, angel?"

I moan at his words and the feel of his cock growing harder inside me.

"Besides, if I'm not in control, how can I make you squirm?" I moan, and he chuckles. "Let me hear you, baby. You like it when I make this pussy gush."

"Oh, Trevor. Yes. Yes, I love when you make it gush." I think I'm delirious with pleasure. I'm clawing at my bed sheets, thrashing my head side to side as I try to fight the pleasure a little longer, but he's too damn good.

"I want it, Peggy. You know when I ask, angel, you don't hesitate."

He's right—my body goes off every time he demands it. I groan, and he continues to work my body, hitting my sweet spot.

He leans down and whispers, "Be a good angel and give me that gush, baby."

I scream his name, feeling my sheets being drenched from my squirting release, and this time, I do black out.

∽

"When you offered to come back, was lounging in the swing bed on my veranda at six in the morning and eating bowls of Adeline's fruity cereal the plan?" The warm morning breeze carries with an aromatic perfume from my flowerbeds off the veranda. So early in the morning, the stillness and quiet makes it so Trevor and I are alone in the world, in this perfect moment.

"You are my plan, angel. Wherever you are, I plan on being there, too."

"Really?" I shove a spoonful of colorful puffs into my mouth. "Can we make the restroom an exception? I think there are some places I need to be alone."

I refuse to make eye contact with him, staring at my front yard and enjoying how bright the morning is. When I hear his chuckle, I still don't look his way, partly because I'm embarrassed and partly because I'm still pissed off.

This morning, I pulled myself from him to go to the restroom, and shortly after, the door opened and Trevor was standing fully naked in the doorway while I was mid-pee. The horror of him seeing me naked and sitting on the pot, yawning and stretching out my sleep, had me screaming for him to get out. He did, but not before I threw the closest object.

He chuckles again. "You have a dangerous arm there. You could have taken my head off with that plunger had I not dodged it. Next time I'll knock."

"Next time I'll lock it."

"It's human nature."

I cut him a side-eye.

"Too soon?" he asks.

"It will always be too soon."

He chuckles once more before going back to enjoying his mixing bowl full of cereal.

"I'll get you there, baby." He shoves more cereal in his mouth.

I stare at him in disbelief. "Why would you ever want to stand in the restroom with me while I'm relieving myself?"

"Because I love you and I want to experience life with you. I want you to talk with me, laugh with me, and share your feelings with me. I want the uncomfortable moments along with the joyous ones." He finishes the last of his breakfast, tilts the large bowl up to his mouth, and drains it before he leans over the side and sets the bowl on the floor.

He then tilts my chin up and gives me the sweetest, slowest kiss. The tip of his tongue slips between my lips, and it's still cold from the milk. We spent most of Friday in bed, fucking like rabbits. I would have figured my body would be too exhausted and well used, completely sated, but it warms up and melts into him. My body will forever welcome him, ready to please and obey.

I reach out with my bowl, trying to feel for the side table, but suddenly my hand is empty and I'm on my back, nestled into a wall of plush pillows. Trevor hovers over me after he places my bowl inside his on the floor. He lifts the hem of my shirt, exposing my stomach, and rubs my skin, barely grazing the waistband of my panties and my underboob as his palm moves in slow, gentle circles, stoking the fires of my desire.

He gives my lips one slow pull with his and stares at me, his soft expression tugging at my heart. "I've never had this. I told you before that relationships were never something I did. I allowed women only a few hours of my time, and when that was over, they were quickly forgotten, blending into the pool of faces I'd never see again."

I try to school my expressions and remain calm. I don't want to hear him reminisce about the many women he's shared space with. Regardless of how short and meaningless it may have been, that image gets stuck in my head and the fire of jealousy burns my throat. I shift to my side, making his hand slip from my skin. I don't want him to know how much I hate this conversation.

He uses the same hand to move my hair off of my face and behind my ear—the best he can anyway, because my sleek, straight style is long gone, sweated out from hours of sex and steamed from our long shower in the wee-hours of the morning.

He plants a kiss on my neck and lets his lips linger there, and smiles against my skin. "Angel, there's a point to be made here. I do love your jealousy, but I hate when I put it there." He licks the skin over my racing pulse. "My point is, I've been just as lonely as you have over the years. You had your friend William to enjoy a dinner and conversation with a few times a month. You shared your life with him, one reason that gets me all up in arms. I had numerous women and shared nothing, and never received anything either. Most times, my body would be there, but my mind would be elsewhere."

"The point?" I say, wanting him to save me from the vise grip of pain squeezing my throat.

"The point is you may have been a virgin sexually, but I was a virgin emotionally. Even as a kid, in my family, emotions were kept under lock and key. They were considered messy, a nuisance, and a show of weakness. My father was a total asshole and my mother became depressed and withdrawn over time, taking with her all the laughter and love I remembered as a child. I've lived so long without emotional connection, love, and life that I'm starving, Peggy." He pulls me closer, and I melt into him. "I'm starving for your touch, your attention. I crave the intimacy of being in a relationship with you. I understand it's new for us both, but I don't want you to start putting up walls, because I will destroy them with my bare hands if need be."

"I'm not putting up walls, Trevor. I just want to pee alone."

He chuckles, wraps me in his arms, and informs me again that he'll get me there.

11

TREVOR

Heaven is the only word to describe my time in Savannah since I arrived. When I left all those years ago, I was leaving my own personal hell from missing my mother and hating my father. I hated him for breathing, for all his fucked-up contributions to my life, and was pissed at Braden for not feeling the same way I did about the old man. The day I boarded the plane, I promised myself I would never return. Now I don't ever want to leave.

Lying on this swing bed, surrounded by plush pillows, while my angel naps curled in the fetal position, has my heart full and my soul at ease. Peggy's veranda is like our own personal paradise, with potted foliage and flowers scattered about and comfortable seating areas atop colorful outdoor rugs. It's like the indoors spilled outdoors.

The French doors in the family room are open, and from where we lay, we have a clear view to the kitchen and out the opposite side of the house. I was thinking when we marry that I would move us onto an estate with a large house we can work on filling with kids, but I can't see taking Peggy or Adeline from this place. Peggy grew up here and Adeline found a family here. I'm now considering adding on, when we need the room.

Before Peggy's nap, I asked her how she sees her life, if she could choose the perfect one.

"The perfect life, my perfect life?" she asks, with eyebrows raised.

"Yes, how did Peggy Jordan see her life when she was a little girl?" I watch her tuck a few loose curls behind her ears, revealing cheeks warm with a pink blush to them before she gives me a beautiful smile.

"Umm, do you really want to know? It's not very exciting. Actually, it's the most boring life on the planet."

"I'm sure it's just as exciting as traveling the world, posing for high fashion magazines."

She shakes her head. "No, it's far, far removed from the life I started out living."

"Then tell me," I say, positioning the pillows behind my back so I'm sitting in an upright position.

Peggy is beside me, sitting crossed-legged, enjoying a glass of iced tea I poured for her. She looks around the yard as if she's trying to picture a different time. She brings her eyes back to me and nestles into the pillows, stretching out her legs and resting her feet across my lap as if she's settling in for a long story. I take her feet and rub them, comforting her.

"When I was a little girl, I saw my life as the one I started out living —traveling the world, posing for high fashion magazines, as you put it. However, after I left that life, I saw my world differently. It wasn't until after my parents died and I was responsible for Clarisse, that my life changed and what I desired changed too."

"Sounds interesting enough."

She smiles at me and tilts her glass up to her lips. I watch her throat move while she swallows, and a bead of sweat works its way down her neck. It pools at the base of her throat before spilling down between her breasts.

"You want more iced tea?"

"No, this is good." She clears her throat and sets the empty glass on the side table. "Okay, so after I stopped modeling and came home, I was able to really appreciate the life my parents had worked so hard to provide for us. While in college, I lived in the dorm, but every time I felt lonely there, I knew I was always welcomed home . Any time of the day or night,

I could make my way back here, sleep in my old bedroom, and remember how safe I felt behind these walls. It made me realize how different I had become after my attack. No other place ever felt right to me after that, and I craved normalcy. You know that loose floorboard at the bottom of the stairs?" I nod. *"Whenever I walked through those doors, I wanted my family to greet me, to come out of wherever with warm smiles and hugs to welcome me back. So I would purposely step on that loose floorboard, and the noise was like my calling card."*

She smiles, wrapping her hands around her chest and arms as if imagining the scene she's describing. *"My mother was always the first. She would come from the kitchen—always the kitchen. She would greet me just as I imagined, with open arms, and offer me something to eat. When I was traveling, I loved watching old black-and-white movies. I liked the simple ways they lived and how all the women were sophisticated. How their hair was always neatly pinned up, but at night they would let loose the pins and their hair would cascade down their backs. I loved that they would serve their husbands and tend to their kids. How everything was homegrown and homemade. That's my perfect life."*

She looks around again and then pulls her long, curly hair from her hair tie, and I watch as the wind flows through it, carrying a wave of chestnut around her beautiful face. She inhales the scent of the warm Southern afternoon and her smile brightens, as if her perfect life is just around the corner. *"If life was perfect, I would be a stay-at-home mom with four to six kids, no more than two years apart. I would want them all brought up in this house, where my husband would love me and protect his family. Where we would eat every meal together, grow our own veggies and fruits to sell at the local farmers' market on weekends. Where I'd carpool and never miss one recital, sporting event, or important milestone in their lives.*

"And when the sun goes down, after my husband and I put our kids to bed with bedtime stories and kisses on the forehead, we would make our way to our bedroom, where I'd submit to his sexual desires. He'd use his body to make me come so hard I must bite the pillow so I don't wake the kids, and in the early morning hours, we would lie together and discuss the day ahead and plans for our future.

"We would take family vacations twice a year, one in the summer and the other at the beginning of December, where we would go up north somewhere to enjoy the snow." Her gaze passes me, the house, and drifts off, worlds away. "We would send our kids off to college from this front porch and welcome them home with their families for every holiday the same way. I'll cook everyone's favorite dish and my husband would carve the turkey with all our grandkids clapping and cheering, begging for the first slice. At Christmas, we'll dress as Mr. and Mrs. Claus while we pass out gifts, and before bed, he'd tell the story of Christmas with the grandkids sitting at his feet, the same way our kids did when they were little."

I stare in awe at Peggy and how perfect for me she is. More than anything I want to be the man she describes in her fantasy. The picture she laid out in living color sparked a fire inside me, and all I want is to start working toward making her perfect life a reality.

I gaze at her while she stares out into the beyond. I'm about to ask her what she's thinking when she moves her legs from my lap and scoots her bottom next to mine, wrapping me in an embrace as she rests her head on my chest. We sit together, enjoying the comfortable silence, both still stuck in Peggy's perfect life.

The corners of my mouth lift, and I feel as if I'm smiling with my whole heart. With her holding me as though I'm going to blow away, I have to choke back my words, fighting not to ask her to marry me. Peggy didn't just lay out her perfect life. She described our perfect life, the one I will give her.

"What is your perfect life, if you could choose?" Peggy's question comes without warning. She was so quiet for so long, I assumed she was sleeping.

"I never gave thought to the notion of what perfect would be like until I laid eyes on you. Standing in the doorway of your kitchen, watching you and Adeline, was the closest I'd ever come to perfection. As long as I have you and Adeline, my life is perfect. Whatever happens, wherever we end up will be perfect because I got there with you." I squeeze her and kiss her forehead. "Thank you."

"For what?"

"For making me a part of your future, your dreams."

"The moment I laid eyes on you, kneeling in front of me in my kitchen, you were the only man who could take that spot." She faces me. *"I love you, Trevor."*

The picture of our life that Peggy laid out will become a reality, and I've already initiated a plan to get us there.

A few hours ago, Peggy drifted off to sleep, wrapped around me. Since then, I've made some calls. I received a full report on the progress of the department audits and yes, it looks as if The Golden Temple is in need of filling several positions. This news is very frustrating. I can't wait to marry Peggy and adopt Adeline, but I don't want to move forward until the casino is stable and this issue pushes my timeline out by several months.

It's a Saturday afternoon, and I'm limited on what I can do to jump on the hiring process, so I add contacting a hiring agency to my growing list of to-dos. I've also reached out to a jeweler so I can find the perfect ring for my angel. The last task is putting my baby inside Peggy, if I haven't accomplished that already.

Peggy has been very emotional lately and the thought of her carrying our child has blood rushing to my cock. If I hadn't kept her up practically the entire night fucking, I would roll her over on her back, spread her smooth thighs, slide my hard piece between her folds, and enjoy her slowly for hours.

Peggy stirs in her sleep, making her T-shirt rise until her ass cheeks are peeking from under the hem. I lick my lips at the thought of tasting her skin and her sweet nectar. My cock jerks in my shorts, and I fist my thickness through the fabric. I give my length one slow pump before palming her ass, wanting to test out the soft squeeze of her flesh. Before I can, my cell blares out the sound of my FaceTime. I left my phone on the table and read Adeline's name on the screen. Talk about a boner-killer.

I walk away from the swing bed while I take her call, so as not to wake Peggy. "Hi, little bird, are you having fun?"

"Yes, I am! We're leaving the park, and my cousins and I played with two puppies and they were biting our fingers."

"Is that so?"

"Yes, and Riley asked Auntie can she and FJ have a puppy, and I want one too! We're going to name them Peanut Butter and Jelly."

"Is that so? Peanut Butter and Jelly?" I repeat, loving their creativity.

She nods and hits me with that smile that has the power to make me move mountains in her name.

I want Adeline to have a beautiful, normal childhood, and if a puppy will give her that, I don't mind, but I do have to talk it over with Peggy. In our perfect life, she never said a thing about a puppy. "Let the adults talk this over first, and I'll get back to you with an answer. How does that sound?"

She squints at the screen as if she's giving my words careful consideration. She looks over her shoulders, and I glance past her and notice two puppies bouncing around the twins' feet. She turns to the screen again, and I see her longing. I almost give in.

"Okay, Uncle Trevor, I'll wait. Just think about how much fun a puppy will be."

"I will, little bird, you have my word."

∽

"Where are we going?" I glance in the rearview mirror at Adeline. She's stretching her neck, trying for a better look at the landscape out her window. "We've been driving for hours."

It's only been twenty minutes since we've left the house. I chuckle and cut a side-eye at Peggy. She's dozed off already. She's been extremely tired these last two weeks since I've returned from Vegas. I catch her napping at odd times during the day. A few times I've left her sleeping while I accompanied Adeline to her classes. She told me her checkup went smoothly, that it was just an annual thing, but my thoughts return to that visit. I know she's getting tired of me asking her about it.

"Uncle Trevor—"

"We'll be there shortly, little bird."

She smiles and bobs her head to a kids' soundtrack. She told me the name but I forgot already. Gripping the steering wheel, I focus on the road. It took me the entire two weeks to find a dog breeder who had three puppies from the same litter, ready for a new home. The farm is a little more than an hour away, but it's worth the travel. Peggy agreed to one dog, but she'll be surprised when we take home the other two. At least, that's what I'm hoping. I turn to her again. She's reclined in the passenger seat, and her head has lolled to her left shoulder. After I bring to the SUV to a stop at a red light, I lift my cell phone from the center console and take a quick photo. She stirs and opens her eyes, I'm guessing because the car isn't in motion.

"We're not there yet?" she asks, and the light turns green.

I press the gas and propel the car forward. I expect her to protest the drive, but she reclines the seat further, settling in to sleep the rest of the way.

∼

"Can we keep them, Uncle Trevor?" Adeline is screaming and laughing. The three rambunctious Yorkies bounce and climb all over her while she lays out on a blanket in the soft glass.

"Yes, little bird, we're taking Peanut, Butter, and Jelly home."

"We are?" Peggy steps in front of me and lowers her voice. "We said a puppy, baby, not three."

"We each get one." I silence her protest with a taste of her full lips. Gripping her hips, I turn her around to face Adeline and the puppies. "See how happy she is?" I whisper in her ear, then blow raspberries on her neck and she squeals and giggles, shouldering me away.

I wrap Peggy in my arms and rest my chin on her right shoulder. We watch Adeline's feeble attempt at keeping her puppies in the crate we'll be bringing them home in. Peggy chuckles against my body before the soft sound breaks through the squeals and puppy barks to reach my ears.

"Is that a yes, angel?"

She turns her head and presses a kiss to my left cheek. "That's a yes."

∼

IT TOOK me two weeks to find PB&J and an additional two weeks to train the little pups from the training pads, to barking at the back door in the mudroom to go outside. Adeline has been a great help with the training, and she's still doing a wonderful job helping to care for them.

I never had a pet growing up and am grateful for Peggy's experience. When we talked about a puppy, she shared the story of how she loss her Pomeranian many years ago. These little pups not only make Adeline happy, but they also keep Peggy smiling. Having the puppies also keeps Adeline busy, giving Peggy a break. She's still really tired most days and I'm conducting as much business with the casino as I can over the phone, working out ways to shelve problems that need my personal attention until I have to return to Vegas.

I'm in the mudroom with Adeline helping her feed PB&J when I hear Peggy's cell phone ringing in the distance. I left her on the veranda where we were finalizing the details of our first vacation together. We decided we'll take the trip next month before Adeline starts her new school. This was a last minute plan, but Peggy was able to secure us a two week stay at a very private, extremely secluded country home. It belongs to Delta Price, Dylan's mother. I never met her but it's very generous of her to allow us the run of her vacation home.

A short while after, I hear my cell ringing and remember I left it with Peggy when I came to help Adeline. I quickly wash my hands, but Peggy appears seconds later with her cell to her ear and my silent cell in hand. I take it and read Jennifer's name on the screen.

. . .

Before I left for the airport, Peggy informed me that the call she received was from the doctor, and she has an appointment in two days that I promised to be home in time for. She hasn't been herself lately, fatigued, moody—more so with me for not only handling my business but trying to handle hers, too.

Peggy is looking to bring in four farmers to work her gardens and the greenhouse. I didn't think what I did was so bad, at first anyway, when I interviewed one of the candidates for a farmer's position. She fell asleep on the sofa after finishing the lunch I made her, and I didn't want to wake her when one of them came to the door. She had already conducted two interviews earlier that day, and I knew she was exhausted.

"Trevor, I can handle my business, you focus on yours. Do you see me camping out in your office with Jennifer mumbling in my fucking ear?"

"No, but you were sleeping so peacefully, I didn't want to wake you angel, and I do have farming experience. I know what to look for, what to ask."

Peggy stomped off the veranda and stood in front of me with hands on her hips, chin raised, and a mean glare in her eyes. She looked me dead in mine before she set me straight.

"This is my business, and I have to feel comfortable working alongside my employees and expect them to take me serious and respect my authority. How can I achieve that if my boyfriend fills in for me because I'm taking a fucking nap?" She storms off with the sexiest sway in her hips. I lick my lips, already thinking of how I'll apologize for my misstep.

"For the record, I never said you were sleeping!"

That incident happened a few days ago, and it took a few days to sweeten her disposition. I enjoyed every minute of it. Finding out my angel is carrying my baby will make me the happiest man alive.

Mr. Spencer picked a fine time to kick off negotiations. I promised Peggy I'd be back for her appointment, but I'm not sure I can keep that promise. My first day in Vegas was spent shut in with a bunch of suits arguing back and forth. After a late-night meeting with Jennifer and the CFO, I'm expecting the road to finalizing this merger a long one. I was told to expect a grueling next few weeks, at best. If I was going to have any chance of making Peggy's appointment, I should have left last night, but an early morning meeting has me texting her instead. I take a deep breath and my phone vibrates. I see a text from Peggy.

My Angel: At my appointment, have you landed?

I stare at her message and try to decide if I should let her know now or later that I may not be home for a few weeks. I quickly decide to wait, but I do have to break the news that I won't be home now like I promised.

Me: I'm sorry, angel. I missed my flight, currently in negotiations.

My Angel: Oh, ok. When will you be home?

Me: I don't know yet.

This would be a good time to tell her no time soon, but I want to hear her voice when I explain. I'm hoping for the best.

Me: Have you been examined?

My Angel: No, waiting on the doctor. I'll let you know.

Thirty minutes later.

Me: Baby, what did the doctor say?

Four minutes later.

Me: Are you still waiting?

An hour later, still no response. I can't concentrate. I have to hear from her so I can find out if I knocked up my beautiful bride-to-be, so we can marry and adopt Adeline, so I can start working on giving her four or six babies, so we can raise them in her family home and see them off to college from the front fucking porch. And I can't call while I'm listening to these assholes go on and on about matters that shouldn't be issues. We have a solid offer on the table. Why are they being so goddamn difficult?

"We've been at this for hours." I stand and walk to the door. With my hand on the knob, I continue. "How about we all stretch our legs, clear our heads with some fresh air, and we'll pick this up after two o'clock."

"We'll be on our way to executing these contracts if you stop playing hardball, Trevor." Mr. Spencer stands and makes his way to my side. He's a tall, portly man with salt and pepper hair and eyes so narrow he constantly looks like he's squinting, even though he's not. "Let's just make this easy." He pats my back.

I feel like breaking that arm he has around my shoulders. He claims we're playing hardball, but his counter terms are fucking ridiculous, and I'm a hundred percent sure he's simply trying to squeeze more money out of me.

"This is business, Spencer." That's only response I give before I dismiss everyone for a couple hours.

"I told you this wouldn't be a walk in the park." Jennifer's the last to stand and make her way to me. She's a short and curvy woman with an authoritative voice.

I rub the back of my neck to alleviate the tension there. "I need some time. I have to call Peggy. She's not responding to my texts."

"Sure, Trevor, I'll be in my office. In the meantime, call Peggy, and try to get a little rest, too."

Back in the hotel's penthouse, I plop on the bed and pull up FaceTime, staring at the black screen and longing to see Peggy's face. To my surprise, there is no answer, and I try once more, only to end with the same result.

I abandon FaceTime and try calling her. I hear her sweet voice on her voice mail, and I almost lose it. I disconnect the call, squeezing the phone almost hard enough to crack the screen or shatter the fucking thing completely. Tapping, the edge of it on my forehead, I send up a prayer that I can keep my cool when I try her again.

12

PEGGY

I'm pregnant!
 I scream the words in my head. Driving to pick up Adeline from her art class, I can't stop smiling. This news really explains a lot—my mood, fatigue, appetite. One thing I didn't experience—which I'm thankful for—is morning sickness. My appointment ran longer then I anticipated. My doctor did an ultrasound and full blood work before finally calling me into his office an hour later to tell me that not only am I pregnant, but I'm further along than I suspected. I'm two weeks late this month, but apparently I experienced intermittent bleeding, which seemed like a period is not the same as menstruation.

I'm actually twelve weeks along, approaching the end of my first trimester. Not only that, I'm carrying not one, but three babies. I was speechless after being told the news, accompanied with the fact that more likely than not, I conceived the first time I had sex. The doctor took the last forty-five minutes explaining possible risks with carrying triplets and to expect a call when the results of my full blood work comes in.

I sat in my SUV in the parking lot an additional twenty minutes, staring at missed calls and texts messages from Trevor.

I'm not sure why I'm hesitating to tell him we're going to be parents. I know he'll be over the moon about the news, but something has me stalling. Maybe it's the fact that he's so busy with work. We've talked about his position as CEO of his family's casino, and Trevor has shared with me that he plans to let the executives and managers who've run the business in his absence continue to do so, but until that time comes, he has a lot of work ahead for him.

I'll wait until he calls me tonight, and then I'll feel him out. I could send a quick text, saying we'll talk later, but I'm sure he'll bother me and worry until then, and his progress with work today will be delayed. I turn the SUV in a parking space and make my way to Adeline's classroom. On the way, I receive another text from Trevor.

Trevor: Peggy you are driving me crazy! I'm going insane not knowing what's going on.

I stand outside the classroom, staring at my phone, and make a quick decision to text back. But I need to keep it short, not giving anything away, but also appeasing him.

Me: Sorry, the appointment went well. Got caught up and now I'm picking up Adeline. We'll talk tonight. Finish your meetings, finalize this merger, and come back to me.

Trevor: How was the appointment? At least give me something.

Me: Good. We'll talk later. [kissy face]

I really hope this works. Waiting another few minutes with no reply, I exhale and enter the building to pick up Adeline.

The rest of my day went by smoothly. Tomorrow is Saturday and our girls' brunch. Adeline and I are meeting Clarisse and Riley, and Rhonda is driving down from Atlanta. I think this is the best time to tell them my good news. Adeline is all talk in the back seat. Today was an abstract art lesson, and she's going on about hearts and circles and how your moods have their own color.

"What color are you right now, squirt?"

"I'm happy yellow, because I'm going home, and when I get

home I'll be excited orange to see PB&J. Then I'll turn loveable red because they kiss my face and jump around me."

I chuckle because she's smiling so wide she actually brightens.

"After they go outside, I'll become hungry green. What's your color?"

"I think…" I take a minute to assess my overall feelings. "I believe I'm yellow, orange, red, and also green." I eye her in the rearview mirror and her smile beams brighter, if that's even possible.

"Like me!"

"Yes, just like you. What are we having for dinner tonight?" I ask because I'm so hungry. I rest a hand on my belly and whisper, "I'll feed y'all soon."

"Pasta!" Adeline yells, and my stomach rumbles.

∽

THE MORNING LIGHT floods my room and I'm tapped awake on my shoulder. Opening my eyes, I see Adeline's smile and I sit up. "Pancakes?"

She nods and I flip the covers from my body. I lazily stroll to the restroom, stretching and rubbing the lingering sleep from my eyes. "How about we do something light this morning, squirt? I promise to order you pancakes for brunch." I try bargaining with her because I may not have time for her usual pancake breakfast. We have to dress, and I want to try calling Trevor. I dozed off early last night. The excitement was possibly too much for me. I texted him before I shut my eyes to explain, but glancing at my cell phone, he has yet to read the message.

"Can I have yogurt and berries, Peggy?"

"Sure."

I knot my hair in a bun to wash my face and brush my teeth. The happy glow on my face I have no control over, and when my belly rumbles I rub it, soothing my little hungry ones growing inside me. *Wow, am I imagining this?* I lift my muscle shirt and lower the waistband of my small shorts, marveling at the slight baby bump I'm sure wasn't there yesterday.

"Can I wear my ballerina dress to eat pancakes?" Adeline calls from my bedroom.

It's not really a ballerina dress. It's a pink and red tulle skirt attached to a white ribbed tank top.

"You don't think it's too dressy for brunch?"

"No." I hear her pad out my room, no doubt going to pull it off the hanger.

I decide to wear something form-fitting to show off my little baby body. I'm so excited, I want to see if my sister notices before I have to mention I'm pregnant. I look in the mirror and smooth the fabric over my hips and fluff my curls, leaving them to cascade down my back. Minutes later, Adeline and I make our way out the house. I'm purposely running ten minutes late because I want Clarisse and Rhonda to see me as I approach our usual table at Honeydew, Clarisse's southern café.

Before pulling off down my driveway, I check for a text but nothing yet. The message is still showing delivered. I frown and try texting Trevor again.

Me: Adeline and I are heading out for brunch. I know the casino never closes, but I hope you're at least meeting-free today so we can talk later.

I stare at the screen and hold my breath, waiting for *delivered* to change to *read*. I give up after a few minutes and head to Honeydew. Whatever Trevor is dealing with, it definitely has all of his attention. Concern creeps up my spine. I'm not sure what to make of his silence.

I wonder what mood color am I right now.

∼

"When did we start dressing up for Saturday brunch?" Rhonda

asks. There are brief hugs and air kisses around the table before we take our seats and the girls rush over to sit at the counter for a slice of pie.

"I woke up this morning feeling radiant and full of love. I was like, why not, this may be the last time I'll be able to fit this dress." I smile, eyeing my sister and Rhonda.

"Full of love? Pegs, this is the most sexual conversation you've ever had with us," Clarisse teases.

"Clarisse, this is the first time Peggy has ever held on to a man long enough for him to put a smile on her face."

"Or babies in the oven," I mumble, because they set that up too damn good, but apparently they didn't hear me. Shortly after, we're interrupted by the waitress serving us our usual starters—coffee and beignets.

"No coffee for me. Let me get hot water and lemon," I order before she walks away.

"Nice, Pegs. I'll have a mug of what she's having," Clarisse says.

"Peggy, before you sashayed your sexy ass through the doors, we were talking about my grandmother's birthday bash this coming spring. We know Clarisse won't be able to make it, with newborns in tow, but how about you? Do you think you can pull yourself from under Trevor long enough to hit the road to Atlanta and enjoy birthday cake?"

Rhonda welcomes the hot mug of deliciousness to her lips and my mouth waters. I think of the list of food and beverage no no's, and I'll miss coffee the most.

"I'm sorry, but come this spring I won't be able to travel, either."

It just hit me that Clarisse and I are a few months apart. The realization spikes my excitement, and I'm about to burst, but I play it cool. The waitress returns with my hot beverage and I take a sip.

Rhonda's frowning, and I know the question is coming… right…about…

"Why won't you be able to travel?" she asks.

I take another sip from my mug. "Because I'll also have newborns in tow." I lift my mug and take another sip, then hold up three fingers. "Three of them, to be exact."

"Peggy!" Clarisse screams.

People from two tables nearby glance over, but I ignore them. I stand and give my sister and friend a better look of my small baby bump.

Rhonda has yet to say a word. Clarisse is on her feet now waddling towards me. Because she's so much shorter than I am, she warps her arms around my waist. I suspect she's tearing up and so am I.

"I'm going to be an aunt?" she asks in a thick voice.

I nod and we're both wide smiles and teary eyes.

"I'm going to be an aunt," Clarisse says. She turns to Rhonda who's standing too, but still has yet to say a word. "We're going to be aunts!" Clarisse announces to Rhonda, as if she wasn't present when I made the statement.

Rhonda moves closer, with a smile and wraps me in a big hug. "Leave it up to you to find a man who shoots three-headed sperm."

"I can't with you, Rhonda," I say but I also can't help but laugh at her crass comment. "Can always count on you to comment from the unfiltered side of your brain."

"When did you find out? How far along are you? When's the due date? OMG, our babies are going to grow up together!" Clarisse bounces on the balls of her feet. I motion for us to take our seats, because the other patrons are looking at us now, and Adeline doesn't know.

"I found out yesterday, twelve weeks, mid-April, but with triplets I could easily deliver as early as thirty-two weeks." I gave quick answers so we can dive into our beignets. I'm starving.

Clarissa leaned toward me. "What did Trevor say? I bet he's over the moon."

I look away and glance at the girls stuffing the last of their pie into their mouths and know I only have a few minutes to explain and change the topic before they return to our table.

"He's in Vegas for business. I haven't told him yet." I shrug like it's no big deal. "We haven't spoken. He's been in back to back meetings, and I don't think he's receiving my text messages."

"You're going to tell him over text?" Clarisse sounds appalled.

"No," I say with an eye roll.

The table falls quiet because we're stuffing our mouths with the warm, sweet, messy beignets. For reasons I don't understand, a zing of anxious energy vibrates by tummy and I have to hear Trevor's voice. I have an urgency to tell him, to have him hold me, hold us—I rest my hand on my small bump—in his arms.

I need his lavender scent to calm me. I pull my phone from my handbag and find his number. His generic voicemail message greets me, and I don't bother leaving a message. I shoot him a text and ask him to call me ASAP. Maybe if he thinks it's an emergency, he'll walk away from whatever meeting he's sitting in or business he's handling right now, to call me back.

"No answer?" Rhonda asks.

I shake my head and grab another beignet.

"Go to him," Clarisse says.

"I can't go to Vegas. Adeline has classes. Not only that, what will I do in Vegas while he's too busy for me?"

"Gamble, get a tattoo." My sister giggles at her own joke while I smack my lips at the thought.

Rhonda set her coffee mug on the table. "You know, that's not a bad idea, Pegs. It can be a short trip. Pop in, say, "Hey, Trevor you knocked me up and because of your King Ghidorah sperm, we're having triplets." Then pop back, but not until you get some loving first. Pregnancy sex, I've heard, is ohmigod!"

"King Ghidorah?" I wait for Rhonda to explain what in the hell she's talking about.

"King Ghidorah…You never watched the original Godzilla?" Clarisse is frowning like I'm some Martian. "Connor made Rhonda and I watch that movie, just as much as Rhonda made us watch every damn Disney movie out while we were growing up."

I frown, still not sure what the heck is a Ghid...something.

"The three-headed dragon, Peggy," Clarissa explained in an exasperated voice.

"I've never seen that movie before. How was I supposed to know that? But Rhonda, you do have a point. I could surprise him with the news in person."

Clarisse and Rhonda both nod in agreement, and I pop the last beignet in my mouth.

∼

I TOOK the first flight I could on Saturday. It landed thirty minutes ago, and I'm now on my way to The Golden Temple. Clarisse took Adeline for the night.

My returning flight leaves Vegas Sunday evening, so that gives me ample time to spend with Trevor without taking him away from his work. I decided to keep on my red, strappy, straight neck bodycon dress from brunch, this way he can get a really good look at what his growing babies are doing to my body.

Sitting in the back of a cab, I check my handbag for the ultrasound picture the doctor gave me, and pass a finger over the images of our growing babies sharing the same space.

In no time, the cab stops in front of the casino, and I send a text to Jennifer. I needed someone to help me with my little surprise, and she was more than happy to assist.

Seconds later, I receive her text that she's waiting in the lobby with the key to Trevor's penthouse. She told me how slammed he has been these last few days, not only with long meetings, but regular casino/hotel business.

I can't imagine the chaos he's dealing with. I do hope the news of my pregnancy will shine some happy light on a bleak situation.

The hustle and bustle of the outdoors spills into the lobby of the hotel. Shows and night clubs are all housed in this massive, but beautiful building. Gold accents are spread throughout the place channeling the name sake very well. I shoulder my overnight bag and push my way through the crowds, which I don't have to endure for long because Jennifer meets me near the doors and escorts me to the private elevator that will take me to the penthouse floor. She's nothing like the tall, authoritative, stoned-faced figure I imagined her to be after our brief conversation.

Jennifer is short and extremely curvy, with a heart-shaped face, pixie-like features, and pouty red lips. My concern for her ability to shoulder the hectic and overwhelming task of keeping order in the life of any person running this place was quickly dismissed when I witnessed the crack of her whip of authority to a few employees during our short walk through the lobby. They scattered about, rushing out the line of fire that is Jennifer Jones.

"I had Trevor called from his room like twenty minutes ago to meet me on the other side of the casino, so you have time to settle in." She hands me the key before she pushes the code in the keypad. "You need to use the key for the elevator to move. Only penthouse staff have complete assess to that floor. I punched in B-Braden's code." Sadness fills her voice on the last words, but she rolls her shoulders back and lifts her head.

"Thank you for all the help." I offer her a warm smile, which she returns, and the doors close after I shove the key in the lock on the elevator panel.

During the ride up all forty-five floors, my stomach twist from excited energy, and I can't wait to see his face. The elevator comes to a stop and the door slides open to reveal lavish surroundings and the Vegas skyline all lit up like a Christmas tree in the background. I drop my bag and make my way to that marvelous view. When I reach the wall of glass, I notice the sliding door and step out onto the massive balcony into the chilled Vegas air.

Closing my eyes, I raise my head and welcome the breeze to cool my heated skin and calm my anxiousness. Turning in a circle I take in fully the large balcony and the comfortable-looking lounge area, and wonder if I can get Trevor to fuck me out here. My core tightens with anticipation, and I rush back inside for my bag so I can shower and get some of my travel off my skin.

When I find the master suite, I push the double doors open and halt at the sight of a half-naked woman draped across his bed. She's wearing a black sheer top that barely covers her large tits, and denim bottoms so short they could be mistaken for panties. I have to force the rising bile down my throat.

"I thought you would never return, baby," her sultry voice purrs, before she catches sight of me standing like a statue in the doorway. "Oh." She sits up, and her large, bare breasts bounce. "When I was sent for, I wasn't told this would be a threesome."

"Sent for?" I repeat, but not as a question for little-miss-eager-to-please to answer.

"Yes. Mr. Duncan needs to release some stress, and that's my speciality." A seductive smile lifts one corner of her mouth.

I cover my mouth, because I'm positive that I'm going to vomit. I rush back to the elevator. I have to get as far away from this place as fast as I can. For a second I forget how the fucking elevator panel works. I fumble with the key, praying that I don't breakdown in this place because I just know it will be bad, really bad, and I'm too far away from home or anyone who loves me. I take a deep breath and exhale, then slowly insert the key with a trembling hand. The doors swish closed and rush me down to the first floor.

When the doors open again, I push through the crowds until the outside noise fills my ears, and I hail a cab.

∼

"Peggy, this just isn't like you," Clarisse says, as she holds me while I cry.

We're seated on the sofa in the living room, and it's been a few days since Vegas.

"I'm so disappointed that he would do something like that behind my back. I was positive that I'd finally found the right man for me. I was so sure of it that I gave him my virginity and didn't think twice about using any protection." I'm hysterical and can't control the hard gasps tightening my abs. Just a few days earlier, I was excited, basking in the thoughts of all my dreams coming true. Realizing it's all an illusion is a hard pill to swallow. "What was I fucking thinking?"

"Wait a damn minute." Rhonda walks in from the kitchen with a platter of sandwiches. "Virgin? Peggy, you were a fucking virgin at your age?"

"Rhonda!" Clarisse says.

We both stare at her, Clarisse wide-eyed and me red with embarrassment. I never wanted that to get out. Ever.

"No wonder you were so fucking uptight," Rhonda mumbles, placing the platter on the coffee table.

"Go the hell, Rhonda." My comeback is weak and lacking any real emotion.

"Hell no, that's where your ass has been the last fifteen years without dick in your life."

"Rhonda!" Clarisse exclaims.

"No, she's right. Before Trevor, I was lonely. I had a chip on my shoulder. My friend, William, was my only regular date. Shit! Why couldn't I have been attracted to him? Why am I always attracted to the worst men in the world?" I wipe tears from my wet cheeks.

Clarisse faces me as we sit side by side on my sofa. She takes my hand and gives it a gentle squeeze. "This was all new and beautiful and you got lost in it, in him." She gives Rhonda a side-eye and then turns back to me. "I know you feel betrayed and your hurting."

I moan. "Now I'm stuck having to deal with his sorry, cheating ass the rest of my life." I rest my hands over my belly and cry harder. Tears stream down my cheeks, but I do nothing to hide them. "I need to get out of here. Everything in this house reminds me of him, of us, and I hate it here." I hate that I allowed Trevor to taint my happy, safe, peaceful place. "How am I going to be able to live here now?"

"You want to sell the house? Maybe we can have a massive estate sale, including men's clothing."

Clarisse's words pull a smile from me, my first one in days.

She kisses my cheek and squeezes me. "I love you, sissy. We'll figure it out."

13

TREVOR

Today marks two weeks of complete chaos. The hiring process is underway and the merger will finally by finalized. We've found common ground, and as I watch the lawyers, assistants, and CFOs leave the conference room with solid instructions to draw up the paperwork, I can finally leave the casino the capable hands of Jennifer and the other executives.

"How do you feel?" Jennifer stands in front of me with her arms crossed in front of her chest. She may be tiny, but standing that way she appears ten feet tall and ready to handle anything. She was invaluable during the negotiations. She is a true beast at her job, and I understand why Braden kept her so close and paid her a hefty salary.

I stay seated, because I feel bad at times when she's forced to look up at me. I stand six foot five inches, and she must be right at four feet eleven inches.

"I'm great, ready to get home and kiss my angel." I sit back in my chair, finally able to breathe.

"She's very beautiful, Trevor. When we spoke last week I pictured her shorter."

"Wait…what? When did you speak to Peggy?"

"When she came to surprise you." Jennifer's frowning down at me like I just lost my mind, but I'm sure my expression mirrors hers.

"Jennifer I don't…"

"Trevor Duncan," Mr. Spencer calls out as he's making his way toward me and Jennifer. "You are one tough sum-bitch, but I knew a visit from one of my more gifted girls would loosen your ass right up." He grabs my shoulder in a tight squeeze and pats my back once. His statement has me out of my chair in a second.

"That was you? You sent that woman to my fucking room?" I roar. I was aware of how Braden conducted his business, but I was not my brother.

Mr. Spencer hands rise in surrender. "I was doing you a favor. Conducting business like this can fuck with your stress level, and Candy specializes in relaxation." He winks at me and realization hits me. I turn wide eyes on Jennifer.

"You said Peggy came last week to surprise me?"

"Yes," she said slowly.

"When did…" Jennifer covers her mouth. I see horror in her gaze and guess what happened. "Peggy went to my room the same time…"

She nods, and I have to grab my chest because I think my heart is ready to explode. I snatch up my phone a try calling her. This is my first call to her since the day she texted me to finish my business so I can come home to her. I've been so fucking busy and exhausted. I remember that night. I thought I smelled her perfume in the elevator, but I chalked it up to exhaustion and missing her so much. To know now that she was actually here and stumbled on a naked women in my fucking bed…

I fist Mr. Spencer's shirt at the base of his neck, ready to connect my fist to his face. But how will that help?

"Get the fuck out!" I yell and shove him away in disgust.

Jennifer escorts Mr. Spencer out of my face. When I think back on that night, the woman tried to tell me something, but I cut her off, commanding her to get the fuck out of my room.

I try Peggy again.

She refused my FaceTime, so I call instead, and get her voicemail. I pull up my text messages and send her a message, when several messages from her ding in back to back. I read through them as they come in, and from the content these must be old messages.

One explains that she was going to sleep because her appointment tired her out. One lets me know they're going to brunch, and another asks me to call ASAP. Her final text makes my stomach clench.

My Angel: We're leaving in the morning. Adeline and I are going to Dylan's mother's house on the vacation we planned before you left. You do remember there is no cell signal or internet, so no more contact after this message. There is a landline. When we arrive, I'll have Adeline call you. I hope your "business" is going well. I told myself I would not be petty in this text message, but you didn't keep your word. If you're wondering what I'm talking about, I WON'T LIE TO YOU, because that would make me you. I wanted this to be different, I really wanted to be different with you, and I thought I could be, but you showed me I was living a fantasy. I love Adeline. I can't imagine my life without her, but she is not mine, she belongs to you. Thank you for letting me borrow her. In the meantime, while you take care of "business," look for another place to live. I can't do this with you Trevor. I thought I was involved with a man who valued me and wanted to be with me, not an asshole who makes promises and say all the right things knowing it's all a lie. I need to put myself first.

∼

ADELINE DID CALL, but I was in a meeting and only found out when we took a break. Her brief message says that they arrived and she was going to play. Peggy took the phone and left me the address and the house phone number, but her words are distorted, and the number she called from registered as unknown, so I couldn't return her call.

I listen to the voice mail over and over again, to no avail. The information needed to find or contact my angel is useless, and I start to believe that the universe is conspiring to keep us apart. I don't have Clarisse's number or much information about Peggy's friends and family to reach out for help in tracking her down.

Frustration builds inside me.

When we return to the conference room, I hurry through the pep talk to the executives and managers I'm meeting with, then rush out the door. On my way to the penthouse for my belongings, I call Jennifer and wish her good luck, thank her for all the hard work she's put in, and tell her I'll be in touch. She wishes me luck before I end the call and head to the airport.

∽

"Welcome to Price Development." The brunette behind the reception desk wears a bright smile that is a stark contrast to my grim mood.

"Trevor Duncan for Dylan Price."

Peggy's brother-in-law's office is my first stop after leaving the airport. Peggy told me what happened recently between Dylan and Clarisse. How Dylan plotted and lied to get her to marry him, and how he had to fight to get her back. I figure if anyone knows what I'm going through—being away from Peggy and needing to fix our broken relationship—it would be him. At least, I hope Dylan is willing to help me. I only need to know where to find my girls. I think I can handle the rest.

I look around the lobby and catch a few women eyeing me. I look back at the receptionist, who seems to be giving me the same interested once-over. She's a young woman with a pretty face, great smile, friendly and warm demeanor—she's the first impression you receive of the company and I see why—but I need her to tuck her gleaming white teeth behind her lips and get me up to talk to Dylan.

"Do you have an appointment, Mr. Duncan?"

"No. I'm his brother-in-law," I lied. "I was in the area and thought I'd stop by."

Her smile slips. It's still bright and cheery, but some of her confidence has dissolved. She nods before picking up her phone. She announces me then listens for a minute before hanging up and instructing me where to find the elevators.

When I reach his floor, another receptionist—this one a guy wearing a sweater vest of all things—it's still ridiculously hot in the south—greets me. "Mr. Duncan?"

"Yes, Trevor Duncan."

"This way, Mr. Duncan. Mr. Price will see you now."

"Thank you."

I follow him to the end of the hall and through large double doors. Dylan stands from his chair and makes his way around with his hand extended. I take his warm greeting as a positive thing, but his grip is firm—a little too firm compared to the first time we met. This may be harder than I thought.

"Good to see you, Trevor, or should I say, good to see you, brother-in-law?" His eyebrows lift in question.

I could waste time explaining myself, but that's not important, and after hearing Dylan and Clarisse's story, I have no doubts Dylan already knows my intentions, so I hop right to it. "I need your help."

"I'm sure you do, but why would I help you?" He gestures toward a chair in front of his desk and then walks to a bar on the far right of his office. "Drink?"

"I'm good, thanks."

"No, you're not. I do realize it's before noon, but I insist."

I raise an eyebrow, wondering what he knows about Peggy and me. He pours amber liquor in two glasses and hands me one before he takes the seat next to mine and taps his glass to mine. Dylan downs the liquor in one swallow, and I follow his lead. The burn coating my throat catches me completely off guard and I cough.

"Not a drinker?"

"No," I choke out, still trying to catch my breath.

"You're looking for your woman?"

"I am, and you're the only one I knew how to contact. Plus I figured you're my best bet at finding her since she's staying at your mother's house."

Dylan chuckles and nods. "You're right. I'm the only one who can help you, but again, why would I help you in your pursuit to hurt my sister-in-law anymore then you have already? Over the past few months, I've seen my sister-in-law in a very new light from when Clarisse and I first got involved. Then—a sweet breath of fresh air. Now—a miserable mess who cries seventy percent of the time." He glares at me. "You see, Peggy cries to Clarisse, and Clarisse brings her concern and tears over her sister to me. If no one has told you yet, I'll clue you in on a little something—I don't like seeing my wife upset. She's five and half months pregnant, and she should always be in a state of bliss, because I believe all the emotions she experiences, our baby does, too."

I understand his message loud and clear, at the same time feeling pissed at myself for allowing this to happen to Peggy. I rest my face in my palms and attempt to scrub away the images of Peggy crying. "I need to know where she is, Dylan."

He nods and walks around his desk before taking a seat there. He places his elbows on the desktop, intertwining his fingers and resting his chin against them. I assume he's deciding whether he should continue, but I'm not leaving here without knowing where to find Adeline and my angel.

"What were you thinking? Was some Vegas ass worth hurting the woman that loves you, that trusted you with her heart? The same woman who welcomed you and your only family into her life? The same woman you named your light, your angel, or blue bird or some shit like that."

I take a deep breath, then I tell Dylan everything from start to finish. He listens without interrupting with questions or adding his own commentary.

When I'm done, he sits back in his chair.

I lean forward in my chair. "I boarded a plane shortly after, and here I am. Now if there's nothing else you want to know, where can I find my angel?"

∽

I've been on this country road for nearly three miles and I've yet to come across this property Dylan told me about. He assured me that Peggy and Adeline are safe out in the middle of nowhere, but I'm not so sure. I don't see much except trees on either side of the long stretch of road I've been driving on.

At the moment I figure I made a wrong turn, I spot a large wrought-iron gate with the name *Delta Dawn* at the top. I park my rental on the short driveway and walk to the side of the gate, where I punch in the code Dylan gave me to unlock a hidden door.

I've changed from my business suit into shorts and a T-shirt, but the heat makes me feel overdressed. I walk a mile and a half up a tree-lined road that ends at a wide clearing.

In the clearing is a mansion surrounded by fields of wild flowers and a lake in the background. I grew up around extravagance and should be immune to the sight before me, but this scenery takes my breath away. It's beautiful, a place that inspires fairytales. I'm half expecting to see a herd of unicorns run from the woods along the water's edge. I scan the area, noticing Peggy's car is nowhere in sight. I assume she parked in a garage out back. Dylan told me that he arranged to have the place fully stocked with every essential so they wouldn't have to leave the grounds.

The sun is high and beating down on my back as I clear the shade of the trees and walk up to the front door. I ring the bell and wait to face the unknown. I don't know what mood I'll find Peggy in when she sees me.

I ring the bell again and wait another few minutes with no answer. I peek through the windows and see no movement in the front rooms. The house is so large, if they are home, they could be anywhere. I leave the front porch and walk the perimeter of the house to check other windows, hoping to catch a glimpse of them before I find a way to intrude.

When I round the side of the house, I hear laughter and a high-pitched scream. It's Adeline, and she sounds happy and excited. I follow the sound of her giggles and pick up the pace, giving an outlet to the excitement bubbling up inside me. When I get closer, I hear Peggy ask Adeline if she wants a Popsicle.

"Yes, ma'am, a red one please," she says.

As I clear the side of the house, I stop short at the sight of Peggy and Adeline surrounded by the clearest blue water I've ever seen. The Olympic-size pool decked out with covered cabanas, an outdoor kitchen, and a covered patio complete with a fireplace surrounded by comfortable sofas. However, neither the picturesque landscape nor the sight of Peggy walking up the stairs of the pool in a tiny red bikini has my heart pounding and my eyes tearing. It's her small baby bump.

I can't pull my eyes from her. Her cinnamon complexion glows under the sunlight, water droplets sparkling like crystals covering her skin. She walks around the pool and grabs a towel to pat her skin dry and wring out her hair. As she does, the puppies run around her feet.

"Peggy, I think the baby wants a red one too," Adeline says as she swims to the edge of the pool.

"You think so?"

"Yes, Peanut, Butter, and Jelly can have ice cubes. Puppies can't have sugar."

"Great idea, squirt. Can you get out of the pool and help me with the puppies, please? I know you can swim, but I have to go in the kitchen, and leaving you alone scares me."

"Okay."

I watch them together, as I did when we first met, but this time she's carrying my baby, making my dreams come true. My longing to be a part of her world is ten times stronger. As Adeline tiptoes toward Peggy, PB&J wagging their tails, run clumsily to her. Peggy picks up Adeline while PB&J bark and bounce around her feet. I stop breathing as panic rises within me. I want to rush up to her and take Adeline from her or scoop up those three little runts, fearing one will trip her. I'm about to call out to her, then I remember how startled she was when I surprised her the day we met. A surge of relief floods me when she stands Adeline on one of the lounge chairs to dry her off and rescue her toes from three nibbling puppies.

Peggy helps Adeline slip on a pair of flip-flops covered in flowers, and they walk hand in hand inside. I move closer and hear them chatting in the kitchen. I walk around the pool and take the seat next to her belongings, seeing a book facedown on her lounge chair. It's a book on the stages of pregnancy.

My breath catches. *Pregnancy?*

I notice her bookmark. She's reading the chapter titled "Now You're Twelve Weeks." If her reading tells me anything, that means my angel was fertile the first time she accepted me inside her. To think that all this time, her body was changing and nurturing our baby.

Dylan's words come back to me.

All the emotions she experiences, our baby does too.

A miserable mess who cries seventy percent of the time.

I drop my head in shame.

"How could you allow this to happen to her? Oh, angel," I whisper. I search my mind for a good enough reason not to end this merger with Spencer and instead ruin his life. This entire situation is just a big misunderstanding I can't wait to clear up.

"Trevor?"

I raise my head. Peggy's alone, standing far away from me. She looks surprised but unsure, and I'm pissed but confused as to whom I'm more upset with: her for keeping her pregnancy from me, me for creating a situation that made her feel she couldn't tell me.

14

PEGGY

"Let me guess. Dylan, Right? He's the only person that would give you the code to the hidden entrance, otherwise you would have had to call from the gate."

He's holding my book, and his gaze leaves my face and moves to my small but noticeable baby belly. I feel so vulnerable and want to cover myself from view, so I wrap my arms around my tummy and look away. Holding our babies growing inside me and staring at his beautiful face has me on the verge of tears. It's been too long since I've seen his face, and now I'm close enough to catch his scent in the wind. I hate him for making me fall in love with him.

"'Now you're twelve weeks.'" He reads the title of the chapter I bookmarked.

I look down at my belly and tighten my hold.

"Don't do that!" His voice booms through the space between us.

My head snaps up at the forcefulness of his tone and the command in his words, and I shoot him a heated glare. He frowns at my arms covering my belly, and I want to snarl the word *mine* at him. He doesn't get the right to claim my babies, because when I needed him and trusted him to be a faithful man, he chose differently.

"Don't do what?" I give the question back in the same forceful, commanding tone. "Don't hold and protect my babies from the man who promised me he was nothing like his cheating, horrible father? I guess it's true what's said about apples not falling too far from the tree." I can't see anything but red. I've been hurting for the last couple of weeks, and he pops up out of nowhere to command the situation? *Not today, not ever.*

His gaze leaves my belly and returns to my eyes. His expression is pained.

I'm too angry to care. "Yes, *my* babies. You had a choice, and you chose random ass or us. You tell me I'm your first priority, yet you chose to sleep with other women."

"Angel—"

"Don't do that!" My voice booms just as loud as his. "You don't get to do that."

I walk away, leaving him there.

I catch Adeline before she can walk outside and convince her it's time for a snack and to feed PB&J. She's been missing Trevor and she doesn't need to see him upset. I don't know what to tell her when they move out of my house for good. I'm not sure what's going through Trevor's mind, showing up after what he did, thinking he'll be able to talk me out of leaving him. But one thing I will never put up with—besides a violent man—is a cheater. I can do bad all by myself.

Addie runs through the kitchen to the pantry and brings out the small bag of puppy kibble. We have the puppies' food bowls on the side of the island, and I hand her the measuring cup and help her serve up the right amount of food for them.

While she's pouring more water for them, she asks, "For dinner, can we eat on the patio then watch a movie, you, me, Peanut, Butter, and Jelly?"

"Can I join?" Trevor's voice comes from the back door.

"Uncle Trevor!"

She jumps in his arms and wraps her little arms around his thick neck. I long to do the same. As crazy as this may sound, I'm starving for his touch, his attention, but I have to be strong. I must stand my ground.

"I thought you would never come back," Addie whispers, and tears break free and spill down my cheeks.

I make eye contact with Trevor, and he mouths, "I can explain."

While carrying Addie, he approaches me and palms my face, thumbing away my tears. His warm hazel eyes plead for forgiveness, and I can tell he's dying inside. I take two steps back, needing to clear my head, because his scent that I love so much, and our skin-to-skin contact, have my body vibrating with rage.

I have to keep it together until later when Adeline goes to sleep. Leaving Trevor and Adeline to catch up and spend time together, I make my way up to my room. I'm sure Addie has enough stories to keep Trevor away from me for hours.

~

I FEEL warm and cozy and moan my pleasure. There's a soft tickle on my skin at the sides of my belly, and I giggle. I try to squirm away to only be nuzzled tighter. I attempt to open my eyes, but my lids are too heavy with sleep. I snuggle further into my plush pillow and sigh with comfort. I love when I dream of Trevor without the cheating. I've been angry and hurting for most of that time. I love when I dream that things are still good with us. I hear his whispers and I squeeze my lids tighter. I can feel my dream slipping away as I'm more conscious of the noises around me.

"I'm so sorry you witnessed that mess, but I promise there's an explanation. Peggy I would never hurt you, never like that."

Trevor's voice is so clear, so close to my ear. I stir and try to move closer to the sound of his voice. I call his name and he answers me with a kiss to my bare shoulder. I settle into the mattress as his lavender scent encases me, and my mouth waters to taste his skin. Something soft, warm, and moist touches my skin below my belly button, and I fully open my eyes.

Trevor's arm is wrapped around my hips and he's placing kisses on my belly, whispering his apologies between each. I'm about to scold him, but he says, "You're mine too, little one."

I hold my breath as I register that he's having a conversation with our baby, and I almost feel terrible for trying to devalue his role in our babies' lives earlier, but I remember he did this to himself and the guilt slips away. I listen as he continues to whisper his one-sided conversation.

"I'm sorry this is the first time you've heard my voice. You're three months strong and I'm proud of you." He believes there's only one baby. "I was told you can feel your mother's emotions, and from what I've learned recently, she's been having a hard time. It's all a very big misunderstanding."

Like I didn't see what I saw in his room, how the fuck can a naked woman sent to fuck your brains out be a fucking misunderstanding. I want to scream at him and kick him away from me, but I don't want my children—as small as they are—involved in any domestic violence.

"You see, little one, my father was never the example of what a good father should be to his kids. He was a great example of what *not* to be as a father, and I make you a promise, right here, right now, that I will always be here for you and your mother." He plants another kiss on my belly.

I have to fight back the urge to yell out. *Liar*!

I feel a shift in the mattress, and Trevor's strong arms wrap me in a comforting embrace, lifting me onto his lap. Everything inside me rages, and I feel like I'm on fire. I want to fight him, fight against his hold on me.

"I never touched that woman."

I close my eyes, fighting against his words, and angry tears fall onto my cheeks.

"I didn't invite her to my bed."

"She said you sent for her."

His lips are close to my ear. "She was sent by Mr. Spencer to, quote, relieve some stress, end quote. I kicked her out of my room and almost fired the entire penthouse staff behind allowing her access to my personal space. Apparently, Braden had certain business practices outside the conference room that made that kind of activity commonplace."

I raise my head from his chest and stare into his eyes. They're sad and his hopeful gaze has me warming up to him, but there are still questions I have to ask. "Why did you shut me out? I understand you couldn't entertain a lengthy conversation with me most times, but a quick reply to my texts would have been nice."

"Your messages were not received on my end until I went to text you this morning after finalizing the merger. Actually, before I tried to contact you, I didn't know you came to see me until Jennifer mentioned your visit. I didn't even know how the woman got in my room until Mr. Spencer mentioned it."

He cups my face in his big hands and passes the pads of his thumbs over my cheeks while his gaze roams over my face. If I wasn't staring into his eyes, I would have missed the change in them. They soften as the worry slips away, replaced with a loving twinkle.

Trevor has admitted to not receiving anything of substance from his manwhore antics and revolving door of hookups. But I too received nothing from my lifestyle.

Modeling had been exciting, but after my attack, I knew I needed a change, a connection to something real. Instead of connecting with the people in my life, I hid away, not attaching to anyone, not even my sister. I raised her after our parents died, but I always saw her as temporary. I knew she would move on with her life, so I did my part and let her go when the time came.

With Trevor, I have no reason to hide away, because he sees me. In this moment, in his arms, I'm finally able to breathe after what felt like a lifetime of pain.

He pulls me into his chest and wraps me in his warmth.

He comforts me in silence, rubbing my arm and my back with

one hand while he rests the other on my belly. When I came to my room earlier, I showered and threw on a loose tank top and maxi skirt before tossing my emotionally drained body on the bed. That's how Trevor found me. I'm still not sure how long I was asleep, so I ask.

"Too long. I tried to allow you to wake on your own, but after Adeline's bath, dinner, and a movie, I was dead set on waking you."

"Where is Adeline?' I ask, frowning because I slept most of the evening.

"She's sleeping. I think after the combination of sun, water, and running around with PB&J, she was exhausted. She was out cold twenty minutes into the movie."

"Oh, what time is it now?"

"After eight. You hungry?"

As soon as he asks, my stomach grumbles so loud, I swear it echoed. My face heats from embarrassment, and I nod.

"Don't do that," he whispers. He lifts my chin and kisses me. I almost moan, but he pulls away too quickly. "You're eating for two."

"No, I'm not." I slide off his lap to my feet and raise my shirt. "I'm eating for four." I giggle at his expression. He frowns in confusion, realization dawns on him and a wide smile splits his face.

"Three? There are three in there?" He holds the sides of my waist and kiss my belly three times. He stands so quickly I take a hasty step back. "Let me get you food." I turn to follow him to the kitchen, but he stops me. "You stay here. I interrupted your sleep, so rest and I'll bring food to you."

Before he leaves, he gives me a hard kiss and a smile that has me wanting to run after him. I take the time I have to relieve myself and wash up a little before changing into a thin sleep shirt. Then I crawl back into bed, gather the covers, and wait for him to return.

I look around the room and stare out the bay of windows with a view of the lake, and I remember when Adeline and I walked the water's edge and a strong warmth floods me. I have to see squirt.

I make my way down the long hallway to her bedroom. When I enter, the scent of her baby powder tickles my nose, and I hold back a sneeze. Ever since she found out about the babies, she's been over-indulging in baby powder. Not sure what that's about.

I walk over to her bed, and the soft glow from her night light allows me to see that she's sleeping peacefully. Her little foot is hanging out from under the covers, so I tuck her in tighter and kiss her forehead.

"She's just as much yours as she's mine."

Trevor's whispered words are carried through Addie's room and sends a shiver through me. His voice always has that effect on my body, and I feel warm between my thighs and welcome that feeling too. I sashay toward him and wrap my arms around his torso, pressing my baby bump against his front. Rubbing against him like a cat in heat, my body purrs and coming to life.

"Slow down, angel. You have to eat, to feed my babies, and we need to talk. There's enough time for that later."

I pout my disagreement, but my stomach grumbles again so loudly I turn to check that Adeline is still sleeping. "Fine."

I pad back to my room. Trevor has set a tray on the table near the window, and I notice a folder is next to two large slices of homemade pizza, a bowl of salad, and a dessert cup full of berries dusted with powdered sugar. My mouth waters, and my stomach flips. Trevor tosses the throw pillows on the bench in the corner and flips back the bedding for me to slip between the covers. He pats the mattress, and I plop down. With him holding the tray of food, I remind him that I'm pregnant, not helpless.

"Angel, this is my first day caring for you and my baby. Please let me have this moment."

"I'm sorry. You're right. Thank you for the food. I'm sure our little ones will enjoy it."

Trevor hits me with his brilliant smile, his entire face lighting up, and the burst of color surrounding his pupils in a golden glow.

"You make it hard for a girl to eat when you daze her with that smile of yours."

"You'll eat and feed my babies, woman." He leans forward and kisses my forehead.

~

"Are we going to talk, or are you just going to watch me eat?" I ask through a mouth full of pizza.

I love making homemade pizza and I deem myself a master, but I'll happily pass the torch to Trevor. I'm tapping my toes on the covers, excited for my next bite. His pepperoni and sausage pizza is orgasmic. Trevor doesn't answer, but he smiles that smile and I suddenly become so emotional. After I lean in and kiss that smile that warms me like the sun, I finish my last slice and frown at my empty plate.

"I can get you another slice. I'm so enjoying your moans and cute humming noises you make while eating."

My cheeks warm. I'm not sure where the embarrassment is coming from, but I pick up the salad fork and dive right in. With a mouth full of salad, I point my fork at the folder. "You wanted to talk?"

I need to get him talking because his stares are doing something to me. Also the folder has been driving me a little crazy with curiosity. I want to finish stuffing my face, but I also have a strong urge to plant my bare ass in his lap and grind down on his thick cock. He smirks and gives me a knowing look, rubbing the neatly trimmed hair on his chin as if he's reading my thoughts. He leans forward, his full lips so close to mine I can feel his warmth pulsing off them, and his eyes are practically glowing as he stares me down. I swallow hard and take a breath, attempting to calm my desires.

"Angel, I promise to take really good care of you, baby. Finish your meal. There's no debating your needs. Food first, fucking after."

I moan as my insides liquefy. "Where does talking fit in?"

"Of course, before I settle between your thighs. I'm planning to make you delirious with pleasure. Having a productive conversation would be impossible after."

"So let's get to talking," I whisper and pass the tip of my tongue over my bottom lip. Trevor follows the movement with those warm hazel spheres, and I want to scream, I'm so fucking horny.

"Do you really believe I would want another woman after having you?"

His question cools some of my heated desires. "Damn, you just jump right into it."

"I'm getting it out of the way, baby, because the scent of your arousal is driving me crazy."

"Oh shit." Just as quickly as he cooled me off, he set me ablaze with one statement. I take a deep, head-clearing breath, attempting to slow my pounding heart. He excites me, but I'm terrified to admit what I went through.

"I wasn't in a good way at all after leaving Vegas," I admit. "I couldn't sleep. I didn't have an appetite, but I forced myself to eat every time Adeline did just so my empty stomach wouldn't make me sick. It happened a few times in the beginning." I look away from him, a little embarrassed by how neglectful I was with my growing babies inside me. "But it wasn't just that. My depression affected Adeline too. She noticed the change in me and told me she was worried I would leave her too, so I told her about the babies, explaining that was why I wasn't myself. I was completely lost and broken over you, and believing it was your choice made me sick with anger."

I push the leafy greens around in my bowl. The room is quiet for some time, the silence making me uncomfortable. I've never felt this vulnerable after admitting how much he can affect my emotions and how I feel about myself. I'm waiting for him to respond, and it's killing me. I take a breath, suck up all my insecurities, and look at him. His smoldering gaze has turned soft, and I feel my emotions bubbling up to the surface.

"Peggy, don't cry, please. You love me the way no one has ever loved me. I was never important to anyone, not really. My father was a bum who only cared about his riches, his women, and his respect in the community. My mother was a lovely woman, she loved Braden and me the best she could, but my father made her numb. Braden and I… well, we had this love-hate thing in our relationship." A frown creased the space between his brows.

I drop my fork and move my lap tray to the nightstand before I crawl to his side and sit back on my heels. I palm his cheeks and smooth the pads of my thumbs along his cheekbones. His right hand covers my small one, and he kisses the palm of my left hand, moving his warm lips over my skin to my wrist before he places another kiss there. He takes a breath. I kiss his lips, needing the connection, to feel what he feels for me. He moans, deepening his kiss, taking control and pouring his feelings into me one stroke of his tongue at a time.

"I don't want you to fight your feelings for me or try to suppress or control them. I want you selfish, desperate, and possessive with my love and attention, because God knows my love is that way for you." He plants another kiss on my wrist. "Peggy, I fell in love with you at first sight. Seeing you in your kitchen, all I could see was the life I've always wanted but never allowed myself to wish for. I never wanted to spend another day without you." He shifts and places his hands on either side of my belly, lovingly caressing me. "Then I saw how much you love Adeline and how much she loves you. I couldn't wait to have a life with you as a family."

I can't breathe, so many emotions are flooding me. Trevor makes me so happy. He reaches around me and taps my feet and I move them from under me and sit my ass on the bed. He tells me to lay back, then he palms my belly, cupping my baby bump, before placing a kiss under my belly button. I stare at him, waiting for his next words.

He slides his palms away, leaving a diamond-encrusted platinum ring with a large center diamond on my belly button. I gasp and prop my weight on my elbows.

Trevor looks at me and holds my stare with intensity and determination. "Marry me and take a chance on a man who had nothing in this world to offer you that you hadn't already provided for yourself. I want to give you the world. I want the privilege to give you love, protection, four to six kids, gardens, a booth at the local farmers' market, family meals, laughter, good night kisses, and vacations. I want to stand on the front porch with my arm around your shoulders as we wave our kids off to college. I want to grow gray and old with you by my side."

"Trevor…" I sit up and take the ring and hold it between my fingers. It's so beautiful. I touch my blue bird pendant and come to the conclusion that Trevor has an eye for selecting great jewelry. I begin to sob, quickly becoming a mess. I can barely catch my breath, let alone speak a complete thought.

Trevor saves me from becoming a babbling idiot by pointing at the folder now by my side. I lift the folder and look his way. Trevor nods at it, and I flip it open. I give the papers a quick once-over. They are adoption forms for Adeline Grace Duncan, naming Trevor Martin Duncan as her father and, to my surprise, Peggy Rene Jordan-Duncan as her mother.

I drop the folder on my lap and cover my face, crying into my palms.

"When are we going to do this?"

He lifts my face from my hands and takes the ring. I extend my hand, anxious to feel the weight of his ring on my finger.

"How about over the weekend?" he says.

"What!"

"That gives us a few days to get the marriage license and pull it together. I'm sure your family wouldn't mind driving out here."

Getting married in four days is…a bit extreme. Honestly, having something small and intimate is perfect for me, since I never really entertained the idea of marriage before Trevor.

"I want us to be married before we stand in front a judge and finalize the adoption. I've waited too long for this, and I refuse to wait any longer. Peggy, I have to have you as my wife. I'm sure as a girl you wanted a big deal made out of your wedding day, and we can still have that, but by the law of this land stretching out across the world, I need it legal and on paper, like, yesterday."

"I'm not going anywhere."

"Really? Then why ask me to get out of your house? Why were you so quick to deny me my babies?" His deep voice is soft and gentle, but I hear the doubt.

I move to his lap, a place I'm longing to remain. "I… I would never keep our children from you. I have part of you growing inside me, these little people who may have your nose." I kiss him there. "Your eyes." I place a kiss on each lid. "Your face." I kiss his cheeks.

I'm inches from his lips, and I can't take my eyes off them. I lick my lips, ready to taste him again. His eyes darken, and I know he's ready for me too.

"Or maybe your lips," I whisper, and take my time kissing him there. His groans spill into my mouth, and I swallow them. I'm ready to take anything else he gives, but I reiterate the situation in Vegas first. "I was angry and I was hurting, and I believed you cheated on me."

"Marry me, angel." His gorgeous face is so close to mine, I can see every angle of his perfection. "This weekend? I can't wait. I've already waited too long. I need you to have my last name, to legally be mine, so I know nothing can take you away." He places a hand on my belly and gives my lips the sweetest kiss. The tip of his tongue caresses the crease of my lips.

"Yes." I whisper my agreement.

"Thank you, Peggy, for making me the happiest man alive."

15

TREVOR

Peggy has my cock the hardest it's ever been, and it's still confined in my shorts. I'm allowing her a few moments to play, to have me the way she wants, before I exert my authority over her, over her body. Peggy's so responsive to every command I give. It's as if she heats and softens around my cock, so when I work her body into a frenzy of orgasmic release, she tightens her hold and milks me of every drop of my seed.

With her hands under my shirt, worshiping my chest and abs, my moans become louder and cock harder. Her greedy little fingers inch closer to the waistband of my boxer briefs, and as she gets closer, my cock pulses, dripping cum. I groan, and she seems to be enjoying herself. The little minx bites her bottom lip, hiding a grin. She arches her back and grinds down on me, and I can feel her hot center massaging the head of my cock.

Her name leaves my lips, a plea for more, more of everything. She answers my plea when her nightshirt hits the floor and her beautiful body is on display for my eyes to feast on. My mouth waters for the taste of her skin, the feel of her hard nipples on my tongue and between my teeth. Peggy's perfect curves are more generous now that she's pregnant. The hourglass shape of her body makes me crazy with lust. Her full breasts bounce and sway with the roll of her hips and the squeeze of her thighs as she works the length of my cock.

I'm barely hanging on to my shit. Peggy shows no mercy, but I refuse to come on myself from her dry-humping me. The idea of her going over the edge this way has me fighting to control myself. I need her to come. I want to watch her come apart in my arms. I've missed the intense expression her features take on when she reaches her climax and the soft gaze she gives after she's relaxed in my arms.

I think it's time I take control, just enough to get her where I need her without dominating her—not yet anyway. I slide my palms around her hips and squeeze the lush flesh of her ass at the same time I take one of her tight nubs into my lips. She lets out a deep groan and throws her head back, and I can feel her hot center pulsing against my cock. I watch her beautiful face, not wanting to miss the changes in her features as she comes down from her high.

"It's been so long since I had such an intense orgasm," she says with that soft, dreamy gaze.

"I love making you come." I'm still fully clothed, still solid as a fucking rock, but I'm content with just holding my angel —for now.

She pushes her hands under my shirt and pulls the soft cotton from my skin. "Now let's get you out of these clothes and your hard cock into my pussy."

"Fuck, you sure know how to romance a guy," I tease, allowing her to undress me.

She ignores my comment and concentrates on undoing my shorts. When she has them open, she takes my mouth with hers, keeping us connected when she slides off my lap so she can yank them down. The flavor of her mouth is sweet and savory and I moan for more.

"Help me," she demands while struggling with my bottoms.

I lift my ass some and she manages to get them down past my cock before she abandons her efforts and straddles my lap. I grab her hips and pull away from her mouth to latch onto a hard nipple, feasting on one before moving to the other. She cries out in pleasure, pushing her breast into my mouth, and rakes her nails down my back. I groan and welcome the pain of her passion and her desire for me. She's clawing at my body with so much desperation, as if she can't get me close enough. I release her nipple with a pop and she groans, but it sounds more frustrated than aroused.

She claws at my shoulders, frantic and practically screams, "Please."

I lower her wet center onto my waiting cock. That first slide of my cock inside her has our moans mingling, filling the silence and making our desire for each other unbearable. Peggy's walls tighten around my cock, pulsing as she gushes her release. I watch the climax roll through her, making her limbs jerk and her breathing labored.

"Fuck, that's a beautiful sight," I whisper and trail open-mouthed kisses down her neck to the swell of her breast. I hold her hips steady and thrust up into her warmth, sucking and nipping at her flesh and nipples.

I'm lost in the feel of her, claiming her harder and faster. Before I know it, I'm begging her to stay, never to leave me, never to take away her heart or her sweet pussy. I'm delirious with need and this position is no good—I must get deeper.

I slide my arms under her legs and stand, cradling her ass in my large hands while I fuck her tight cunt. She bounces her curvy ass off my thighs, taking what she wants. Peggy usually yields her sexual aggression and melts into me when I dominate her body, but not this goddess in my arms. Her desire is so strong, she's refusing to back down. Instead, she's handling me, and I'm not sure she realizes she's doing so. She's squeezing the shit out of my cock, riding me just as hard as I'm thrusting inside her.

"Give it up, angel," I growl and squeeze her ass, slamming my cock into her.

She shuts her eyes and lets her head fall back on a scream while shifting her bottom, and the change in position throws me into the most intense release. I brace myself with one hand on the wall behind her and nuzzle my face between her large breasts, licking and sucking her flesh.

I'm lightheaded while leaning into Peggy's lush curves, attempting to steady myself. She's wrapped around me, and I still feel the light kisses her sweet cunt gives the tip of my cock and I want to kiss it back. I make my way to the bed with as much strength as I can get into my weak muscles and try not to drop her on the mattress. When she's comfortable, I spread her slick thighs and latch onto her hard clit, kissing her there until she's shuddering under me, consumed with another release.

～

"Slow down, little bird, the ceremony will be starting soon."

"Okay, Papa," she yells back to me.

A few days ago, Peggy and I sat Adeline down and shared our good news about the adoption and our wedding. I wanted to wait until after Peggy and I were married to tell her about the adoption, but Peggy disagreed. She said that us getting married has nothing to do with Adeline's adoption, that she would've be adopted regardless. She said us getting married was an added bonus, not the other way around.

When asked how she feels about her father's request that I adopt her, Adeline smiled and asked, "Can I call you Papa?"

I blinked back tears, but holding those tears at bay was nearly impossible after sharing the rest of our news. Adeline's joy was overwhelming, and her bright, innocent eyes sparkled with tears as she confessed to constantly wishing for Peggy to be her mommy, because "Peggy is the only mommy I ever had and will ever want."

Adeline and the twins dart down the back staircase to the kitchen. The pale yellow tulle of her full skirt trails behind her like a flash of sunshine, drawing a smile from my lips.

That same night, after convincing Peggy to go relax in a hot bath, I tucked Adeline into bed, and she asked me about the upcoming wedding.

"Everyone will be arriving in a few days, little bird. We have some planning to do, and you have to get a new dress."

"Awesome! Can I wear any color I want?"

"You sure can. How about we surprise Peggy and take care of that tomorrow? That way she can rest and I can take you on our first Papa-and-little-bird outing. How does that sound?"

She twists her lips up and scrunches her little nose while she squints her left eye, giving my suggestion some major consideration.

I chuckle at how cute her little face looks and ask, "What's the verdict?"

"Do you know how to shop for a five-year-old?"

I chuckle again. "Truthfully, I have zero experience shopping for a five-year-old. But…" I halt her attempt at a protest. "I'm a fast learner and determined to do a good job."

Her gaze is serious when she says, "Okay, Papa, but I think maybe we should get Mommy her favorite dessert too. That way she'll be happy even if you get it all wrong."

I throw my head back, laughing a full-body laugh, and it feels so good. I have never been this happy, and strangely, I have my brother to thank for this moment, for trusting me to care for his daughter. I stand from my kneeling position at the side of her bed and place a kiss on her forehead. "Smart girl."

I whisper a good night and sweet dreams before closing the bedroom door.

Shopping for Adeline's dress was a learning experience, and one thing I learned was that all women, no matter the age, are the same when shopping is involved. I claimed to be a quick learner with determination, but after hours and hours of visiting one girlie store after another, I quickly learned I'm not cut out for such shopping, and I'm very determined never to do it again.

I hear Adeline's giggles from the stairs, and I feel my heart warm. I rest my right palm over my heart, knowing that I'll endure it again, anytime, and all Adeline must do is ask.

I continue down the long hallway toward the room Peggy and I have been sleeping in. I know it's empty—unlike the rest of the house, which is full of family and friends, none of which are mine. The only other family I have couldn't make it, but I was finally able to talk to my best friend Terry last night. He gave me grief about my upcoming nuptials, and I let him have it, only because I knew it was all in good fun. He's more than aware of my feelings for Peggy.

The ceremony will be starting in an hour, and I'm desperate for a few quiet moments alone. I want to reflect on all my blessings and maybe have a one-sided chat with my brother. Marriage never crossed my mind before meeting my angel, so I never considered that Braden wouldn't be standing by my side. I missed his wedding. I missed so much, and right now, I'm wondering if this is how Braden felt on his wedding day. I'm not nervous about being married to Peggy—shit, she's the only thing I'm sure of. I'm nervous… no fuck that, I'm out of my mind afraid I'll mess up.

I'm not familiar enough with this house to know where I can go to collect myself, so I go to the only place guaranteed to give me some peace of mind. On the first floor, I pull an armchair down the hallway and sit outside the master suite door, my eyes closed as I absorb the sound of Peggy's laughter coming from inside.

"She won't get away, dude. I think she's fully committed to marrying you today."

I open my eyes at the sound of Connor's words. He and Dylan are approaching me with grins, and Connor has an extra pep in his step. I smile and stand from my post to shake their hands.

"Don't pay him any mind. If I was in your shoes with Clarisse, I would have locked her in her house until our wedding day," Dylan says.

"This waiting is for the fucking birds," I admit. "And knowing that in less than an hour, she'll be mine completely has my anxiety spiking to an all-time high. It doesn't help that I haven't seen her all day. I'm losing it. Hearing her voice helps."

"News flash, gentlemen, you already got the girl. Stalking is completely uncalled for." Rhonda pushes through Dylan and Connor, fisting her hands on her hips.

I watch their interactions with one another and notice that Connor gravitates toward Rhonda. He towers over her. He and I are the same height, Connor has leaner muscles. If I had to guess, I would put Rhonda at five feet on the nose. In heels she's barely at Connor's shoulder.

"I'm sure Delta has something you men can move around for her. It makes no sense wasting all this manliness just standing around," she says.

"As long as Peggy still carries the name Jordan, I'm staying real close. The last time I left her side, someone fed her the notion that being away from me was a necessity for her mental state." I shake my head and sit back in my chair outside the door. "I'm staying put until the ceremony begins."

Rhonda frowns, and Dylan chuckles. I smile, crossing my arms.

Rhonda moves toward me while pointing a finger. "You know, I like you, Trevor. Anyone who can put a smile on that woman's face is all right in my book. But let's get one thing straight—I will never apologize for advising her to put herself first." She moves past me and grabs the doorknob. "Just because you love her and she loves you is no guarantee you'll stay or that your heart will always belong to her."

Connor lets out a frustrated sigh, and I see something pass over her eyes, but it's gone before I can grab onto it.

She glares at Connor before saying, "Words are cheap, and actions speak louder."

She opens the door and ducks inside. I hear the lock turn right before Connor pulls on the knob.

"Son of a bitch," he growls and walks away, his expression a mixture of pain and anger.

I don't know their story, but I can tell there are some deep-seated issues and I want no part of it. Shit, I think I've witnessed too much already.

I glance at Dylan, who shrugs and says, "Their shit existed

before I was part of the family, and I will never get involved with that mess. It's hard enough to keep my wife out of it.

Dylan looks exhausted, and my heart goes out to him. He loves Clarisse and would do anything for her. From what I've seen, Clarisse would do anything for her sister and best friend, which puts Dylan in a tough spot.

I stand again and rest a hand on his shoulder. "I understand what you mean. Sorry about the last month."

"Thanks, but don't think you can come out of this unscathed. Those women in that room would do anything for each other. Peggy has always been the backbone, and I'll bet my life she always will be."

16

PEGGY

A pounding on the door has me afraid Trevor might knock the thing off the hinges. "Thirty minutes, angel. We start in thirty. I'll see you at the altar, Mrs. Duncan."

His romantic whimsy melts my heart. Now I'm overly anxious to get this exchange of vows over with so we can start living our lives as man and wife. The thought of becoming Mrs. Trevor Duncan makes my pussy drip and my knees weak. Trevor is more than I could have asked for. He's passionate, sweet, considerate, and strong in mind and body. He's gentle and has the patience of Job where Adeline is concerned—who am I kidding, his patience is put more to the test with me than Adeline any day—and for that I send up an abundance of thanks to the Almighty Father.

I walk to the bedroom door and call out to Trevor.

"I'm still here, angel." His voice is soft and low, as if he's leaning into the door.

I place my hands on the door and rest my forehead on the cool wood. "Trevor?"

"Yes, angel?"

I smile because I know he's leaning into the door too. Even though wood is separating us, his body still gravitates toward mine. "See you in thirty minutes."

"You better, or I'm coming back and ripping this door off the wall."

I feel his words in my core. I tighten the silk robe around my waist and smooth my palms over my baby belly. It's all I can do not to fling open the damn door that separates me from my man.

I take a deep breath and turn to Clarisse and Rhonda. "Come on, y'all, let's get the dress on and this wedding over and done with. I'm done with this waiting and with this room."

In six seconds flat, my silk robe lays discarded at my feet and my wedding dress is perfectly in place. I grab my simple bouquet and head toward the door, I stop and turn when I notice Clarisse and Rhonda are rooted in place with wide eyes and raised brows.

I slap the palm of my left hand on my thigh. "Come on, come on. I've waited my entire life for this man, and I'm not waiting another second." I wave them to go ahead of me out the door. "Besides, I'm too horny for this shit."

EPILOGUE

Peggy

Trevor is more than I could have ever dreamed. He's perfect. Shortly after we returned to Savannah, he surprised me with our family stand at the farmers' market, which he named "Peggy's Homegrown Goodness."

My dreams are well on the way to becoming my real life and I'm excited, thanks to my handsome, sexy husband. He's in full support of my goals and even offered to supply my stand with his homemade lavender shampoo cream, but I turned him down. When Trevor asked me why, I told him that he's the only man in the world who smells so delicious and I want to keep it that way.

Ever since Trevor found out that he'd knocked me up with triplets, I swear his goal is to keep me from doing anything more than feeding my face and lounging. The only other responsibility he allows me is caring for Adeline. Even then, he's up before the sun every day, making us breakfast and chauffeuring her to school. Then he picks her up and it's off to ballet Monday, Wednesday, and Friday. On Tuesday and Thursday, it's art class and Saturday is soccer. She has a full schedule. I always tag along, but I haven't been behind the wheel once since I said "I do."

It's now December, and we're packing for our trip to Colorado, our first family winter vacation. I was surprised that Trevor was letting me pack—until he sets my ass in the rocker in the corner of our room and turns the volume up on the soundscape channel.

"I thought I was packing," I say with a pout. He smiles at me, and I want to smack him for being so gorgeous.

"You are packing, angel. You're packing around precious cargo, and right now, you need to rest. Today was a long day for you and Adeline. I saw all the bags brought in from your little shopping trip with your sister."

"It wasn't that many bags, babe. Besides, the personal shopper you and Dylan hired did everything. I swear you guys are spoiling the girls." I giggle when I think of Riley and Adeline, armed with juice boxes and sitting next to Clarisse and me as they yayed-or-nayed outfit choices. "The most work I did was keeping up with a couple of five-year-olds."

"More than enough." He kisses my lips, then bends and places three kisses on my larger-than-life belly.

I smile and shake my head, but inside, I'm melting. I love when he makes a fuss over me. I sit back in the rocker and rub my belly, attempting to sooth the little ones nestled inside. They're always the most active when Trevor is around, no matter if it's day or night. All it takes is for them to hear his voice and my stomach quivers from their somersaults. It's so difficult to get comfortable with all the activity.

"Babe, do you think you can calm your offspring so I can enjoy this relaxing moment?" I ask. "I'm a hundred percent positive they're girls."

A proud-papa smile splits his face. "Why do you say that?" He moves my hands away and picks up where I left off, rubbing my stomach.

"Because only girls go nuts over their daddy." I can see he's giving my logic some thought, then his smile fades into an intense frown. "What is it?"

"Four daughters?"

For a minute, I'm worried about which he would prefer. Not that his preference would change anything, but I never asked if he's hoping for boys or girls.

"We may want to rethink ballet and seriously consider mixed martial arts," he concludes.

I cannot suppress my fit of laughter while I shake my head. I wouldn't be opposed to my daughters learning some self-defense, but the fact that he's contemplating that is funny considering he treats Adeline like a delicate princess. She only signed up for soccer because Riley joined the team. She enjoys playing, but I don't believe she would have joined on her own.

"Or maybe they're boys, ready to meet the man who will teach them all they need to know to be great men one day."

His smile returns, but it's a different smile than the one he gave when I mentioned girls. I'm guessing he's thinking about his brother, and he proves me right when he whispers against my stomach. "You boys are going to look out for each other always."

I place my hand on his cheek, and he meets my gaze. I can see the worry in his eyes. "They will, baby, I promise."

His proud-papa smile returns, and Trevor slides his hands under my nightshirt, lifting it to palm my belly. He presses his lips to my skin and remains that way for several minutes. "I love you, Peggy. You're my angel, my wife, the mother of my children... Forever, I'm yours."

Also by Garden Avenue Press

Honeydew (Southern Seduction #1) by S. Taylor

I'm Yours (Southern Seduction #2) by S. Taylor

Without You (Quicksand #2) by Delaney Diamond

Love Rekindled (All or Nothing #1) by Nyora René

Ready for Love (All or Nothing #2) by Nyora René

The Thick of Things (In Medias Res #1) by J.L. Campbell

When in Barcelona (International Romance #1) by Avery Aston

Do Over (Brooks Family #2) by Delaney Diamond

Wild Thoughts (Brooks Family #3) by Delaney Diamond

First Love Second Chance by Chanta Rand

∽

Visit us
Website: www.gardenavenuepress.com
Twitter: @GardenAvePress
Facebook: www.facebook.com/GardenAvenuePress

ABOUT THE AUTHOR

S. TAYLOR discovered a love of storytelling at the age of twelve. She would entertain her cousins with exciting adventures and tales of young love, which changed over the years from telling tales at sleepovers to writing several short stories.

For S. Taylor writing remained a hobby until 2009 when she decide to share this love with others. She writes love at first sight romance novels full of passion, erotic moments, and emotional conflicts with a satisfying happily ever after ending. She is a Texas native, wife, and busy mother of five daughters. She spends her free time mediating sibling arguments, relaxing with yoga, and discovering new and tasty vegan dishes she enjoys cooking for her family.

www.staylorromance.com

twitter.com/s_taylor2013
instagram.com/s_taylor2013

Made in the USA
Middletown, DE
25 February 2019